Tropical Trouble

Winter Hayles

Published by Winter Hayles, 2018.

This is a work of fiction. Similarities to real people, places, or events are entirely coincidental.

TROPICAL TROUBLE

First edition. September 27, 2018.

ISBN: 979-8201114701

Written by Winter Hayles.

Also by Winter Hayles

Tropical Trouble
Caine: Redux Edition: Bad Boy MC Romance

Tropical Trouble

by

Winter Hayles

Tropical Trouble

Chapter 1

Oswald

Oswald was going to kidnap his very first billionaire.

Finally.

Oswald stood on the deck of the Unsinkable II, and grinned into the wind. Beside him, Reeka, his right hand man, was steering the boat toward their next destination. It wasn't even nine in the morning, but they had already accomplished much in the last twenty four hours. There had been little short notice that the target would be in the area, and a mad scramble was the result.

Oswald shook his head once. Such was the way of his work. Little notice, little time to prepare, and little consideration for the long list of things to be aligned for the job to actual be a success.

But it would all be worth it.

"There it is," said Reeka. His brow was furrowed with concentration, and perhaps a little fatigue. Oswald considered him a good lackey. Reliable. Not a whiff of complaint when things started to move quickly. Always reliable. Of course, even as a right hand man, Reeka was more than aware of the potential reward at the end of this little endeavour.

Lifting a small pair of binoculars to his eyes, Oswald looked in the direction Reeka pointed.

The profile of an island mottled the blue horizon, like a long dark beast pushing itself up from the depths of the sea.

"Yagenda," Oswald said. It was not a question. Even though he had never set foot on it, he had studied every available detail of the place that he could in the last several hours.

It was the intended destination of his target, and so now it was Oswald's. But seeing Yagenda, now, in all its South Pacific magnificence, gave a sort of solidity to what they were about to do.

What he was about to do.

"Kenneth!" he called out. "Front and center."

From the below, a tall lanky man emerged from the open hatch. Even though the open area bridge was well covered from the blazing, morning sun, Kenneth squinted. Long hours of staring at monitors, no doubt.

"Yes, sir?" Kenneth asked.

"Any word, yet?" Oswald asked the group's technician. Although Kenneth could fire a gun as well, if not better, than the rest of them, the skinny man's magic with anything electronic made Oswald think of him as a techie first.

Kenneth rubbed at his eyes, and shook his head. "Not, yet. Neither one has arrived at the harbor."

Oswald frowned slightly, and blinked briefly up at the sun's location. Still too early. But that was fine. Things were almost in place. "Okay," he said. "Keep on it."

Kenneth nodded once, then vanished into the maw of the boat. Below, were all of the accouterments of a lavish speed boat like this was expected to offer. Kenneth, with his array of gear and monitors, was set up in the dining area, claiming its table for himself. Once word arrived that the target was in play, things would get a whole lot more hectic.

Just the way Oswald liked it.

He felt a surge of adrenaline. The anticipation was building. Time for yet another double check.

"Are the assets in position?" he asked Reeka.

Reeka nodded. "All good, boss. Arrived before us. Everything is as tight as can be. And then some."

Oswald nodded, but did not feel relieved. He had attempted to cover all his bases in the small amount of time they had, but he felt that it might not be enough.

The billionaire, Paul Morgan, was known for his vast intelligence, and business cunning. But Oswald did not think he had the toolkit to deal with being snatched up off a tropical island. Especially when he would not even be expecting it. All indications was that he was alone on Tarangia, the main island. But rich people can be paranoid. Especially very rich ones.

Apparently, Paul Morgan hadn't learnt that lesson yet.

In a few short hours, he was about to.

Reeka looked at the radar readout on a monitor. "Coming up on position one."

Despite trusting Reeka's professionalism, Oswald found himself glancing at the radar. They had arrived at the coordinates.

"Cut the engines," Oswald ordered. The engines burbled and died. Their constant grumbling over the last two hours were now replaced with the hard slapping of ocean waves against the boat.

Reeka visibly relaxed a little. For the first time he allowed himself to sit in the captain's chair. The holstered pistol on his shoulder strap shifted with the movement.

"It will be all good, my friend," Oswald told him. He could tell when his long time partner was getting nervous. This was a very big score for them. So big, it could very well be their last.

"I know," said Reeka with a slight smile. "I just have... how do you say in English? Bees in my stomach?" He picked up his covered mug of coffee and took a sip. He grimaced. It was cold.

Oswald laughed. "Butterflies. Butterflies in your stomach. That is okay. I have them, too. Go get some more coffee. You need the caffeine infusion. I got the helm."

Reeka nodded, and took his cold mug down below for a much needed refill.

Oswald stood before the ship's wheel even though it was unnecessary. They would not be moving from this spot for a while. From this vantage point they could easily monitor any ship approaching Yagenda from the main island. And, unless someone had direct business with an empty private island, with its abandoned resort, there should be none.

Except for a billionaire.

Billionaire.

He grinned at the potential size of the ransom they will get for Paul Morgan. Not billions. Impractical. No, he would settle for several hundred million. Now that would be worth it. No more nickel and dime jobs. Just settle himself somewhere nice and hot.

This was a far cry from his early days in the American east coast. Running crews for various bosses and organizations. Over the years, he had developed a reputation for kidnappings.

Kidnappings where very lucrative. Snatch someone important enough, and get paid accordingly. He always kept the targets to the criminal underworld. Less of a pain. No police to deal with, and the money for the ransoms were always available. He always insured his targets had rich backers. Rarely did anyone get hurt.

Or killed.

Paul Morgan would not only be his first billionaire mark, he would be his first real civilian, too. No criminal organization to tangle with. Just his big fat bank account.

He checked the horizon again with the binoculars. Nothing. Not that he was expecting to see Mr. Morgan approaching, yet. But once he did arrive Oswald was more than ready for him.

Initially, Reeka was in favor of snatching him at sea. But there were too many factors that put the plan at risk. What if another boat came by? What if Morgan didn't stop and his boat was faster than the Unsinkable II? Shooting was absolutely not an option. Can't extract a life-time of wealth from a corpse.

No, grabbing the billionaire while he was flat footed on the island, looking at a resort he will never own, was the safest course of action. Reeka eventually agreed, as he almost always did.

Now they just had to wait. Mr. Morgan would deliver himself into his hands soon enough. As for the realtor's representative unfortunate enough to be taking Paul on his tour? So be it. That person would either be a hindrance, or a bonus and would be dealt with accordingly.

Besides, how much trouble could a glorified island tour guide be?

Chapter 2

Lydia

"Buy him chocolate. Billionaires love chocolate!"

Lydia Jennings paused in her shopping, basket full of goods in one hand, and scowled down at her smart phone's image of her sister. "And what do you know about the eating habits of billionaires, Mary? When did this become a thing with you?"

From the other side of the planet, in New York City, Mary allowed herself an expression of confusion. "Well, everything!" She blew her nose into a tissue. "I'm not just laying in bed, sick, just so you can prance around in the tropical sun by yourself. I've been doing research."

Lydia rolled her eyes, and somehow managed to take a bag of peanuts off a shelf and place it in the basket.

The clerk from behind the counter asked, "Need some help, ma'am?" He looked pointedly at Lydia's basket stuffed with snack food of various kinds.

"No, thank you," Lydia said. "I'm almost done." She moved deeper down the aisle. The selection of goods in this tiny store was even more limited than she would have expected. Not that she expected much. But, when you have a potential client like Paul Morgan to cater too, you did what you could.

Lydia switched off the phone's loud speaker and held it to her ear. "Do you have to announce to the world who I am meeting today? Can that be a secret please?"

Mary blew her nose, again, honking in Lydia's ear. "Why? It's good advertising, isn't it? What if people need to know we serve billionaires? They might know a billionaire and refer us!"

"Not this time," Lydia said. She was aware of the certain level of privacy Paul Morgan had cloaked himself with. Starting, and operating giant Internet companies made him rich at a very young age. Very, very rich. But he obviously didn't appreciate the attention such wealth brought him. Hardly any images of the man existed that she could find. Which, in this day and age, was kind of a miracle.

Not that she minded. He was a client, and even though his representatives didn't state as such, privacy would be provided as best as Lydia could do. She just didn't need Paul Morgan's name shouted about for all to hear by her sister.

"This time," Lydia said, "we keep things quiet. It's bad enough we had such short notice. Maybe that's a good thing. No time to advertise what we're up to." She and Mary had built up their Realtor business to the point that they could start representing big, international properties. They had people to handle the local listings, but the Jennings sisters would handle anything overseas.

Preferably warm. With lots of beaches and tanned, hunky men.

This resulted in their first big call. Someone was very interested in an old resort on Yagenda island, long abandoned by some bankrupt conglomerate. The listing price was huge. Colossal, even. Which meant the commission was a sizable percentage of colossal. Of course, Lydia and Mary jumped at the chance. But with Mary sick, Lydia had to handle it on her own.

She grinned. "How you feeling, anyway?" She tried not to sound too smug.

"How do you think? Like I'm on the edge of death!"

Lydia went to the front counter and started to pull things out of the basket for the clerk to register in. She spotted a display of chocolate bars to one side.

"Look, I'll give you an update when I can."

"Call me from the island. No. Call me and tell me how handsome he is! He's single! Dammit! Why do I have to be sick?"

"Because you're the lucky one," Lydia said, and almost cackled.

"Fine. Just keep me updated. It's the only thing keeping me alive!"

"Uh huh," Lydia said, and caught herself rolling her eyes. She then glared at the display of bars, and grabbed a big handful to put on the counter.

"Did you get the chocolate?" Mary whined into her ear.

"Nope," Lydia said, and hung up.

Outside, she was slightly relieved to find her taxi still waiting for her. Not that she really expected him to take off with another tourist. There really weren't many around.

I'm to used to New York taxis, she thought, as she piled the bags of snack food into the back seat. She noticed the driver leering at her, and glancing down her dress. Thankfully, she was wearing a bikini underneath.

"Help, you, miss?" Mr. Leer asked. "Pretty thing like you shouldn't strain yourself. I can help with that."

Lydia managed a laugh as she got in and slammed the door. "No, thanks. I can manage."

"I don't doubt it," he said, and grinned.

Ah, geez. "Take me to the pier, please." She wanted to rip a strip out of the guy, but for right now, she just needed to get the boat ready.

"Okay, then." The driver said, with obvious disappointment.

As they drove, Lydia started shoving bottled water, and soft drinks into the little cooler she had the foresight to buy on her arrival at Tarangia. She had arrived on an overnight flight, checked into the hotel, showered, and grabbed her work stuff before leaving to start her day. She had told the hotel staff not to expect her back until well after dark.

No rest for the weary. Dollar bills danced before her vision. Some things were just worth losing a little sleep over. She can catch up later on a well paid for vacation. A long one. The commission would guarantee that.

They drove at a moderate speed down narrow windy island roads. Houses of various sizes and costs, passed her vision. Most of it poor.

Well, at least they have the sun year round. This weather beat the hip deep snow back home by a long shot.

She checked the time on her phone. It was going to be tight, but if the ship her company had booked was already prepped, and fuelled she would be good to go, once Paul Morgan arrived.

Paul Morgan. Single.

Thanks, Mary. I didn't need to be reminded of that.

Lydia had recently dumped her loser boyfriend, Terry. It was such a bad break up that she resolved never to date another

Terry, again. Ever. All Terry's in the world were completely off limits.

"So, where are you going today, with all that food?" the driver suddenly asked.

"On a boat," she said. She was on the verge of offering to pay this man double fare just to shut up.

"Ah, a boat!" he said in the manner a child might when finding a prize at the bottom of a box of teeth rotting candy. "As an islander, boats are second nature to me. I can help. Maybe be your captain."

"No, thank you. I have one already." No need to get into it with this guy.

The man made a tsk tsk sound and shook his head with exaggerated disappointment. "Ah, to spend the day on the sea with a beautiful woman like you would be something a man could treasure for the rest of his life."

Laying it on a little thick, aren't ya buddy? She thought. Outwardly she just laughed, but politely. She appreciated the compliment. She just didn't need such a compliment today, of all days.

"Thanks, but I'm meeting my boyfriend." That was a good lie.

"Ah, lucky man, then."

He was, she thought. He just didn't know it. The fool.

Mercifully, before the driver could make another impassioned go at her, they pulled up to the pier's entrance. Through a long chain link fence could be see dozens of boats, with the vast ocean spread out past the horizon behind them.

Lydia paid the driver, gathered up her day bag and the cooler, and hopped out. As she walked away the driver called out, "Don't sink, now, baby girl!"

Oh, please, she thought. The cooler was a little heavy, and the hot morning sun was beating down on her. Already, she was starting to sweat up a storm.

It will make for a great first impression.

Next to the pier's gate was a tiny building with the sign above saying 'Harbor Master'. She made her way toward it, and pushed her way through its glass door.

After some muddling with the harbor master, she managed to pick up the ship booking Mary had made for her. It was a forty footer, with high powered engines, and already fully fuelled. Considering the price it had better be.

As she was leaving the little office the harbor master called after her, "Don't you need a captain?"

Lydia simply rolled her eyes and made her way down the pier.

She gazed in amazement at all the beautiful boats docked here. She envied the owners of each one, even the crappy little sail boats. At least someone got to own it and use it here in this stunning area of the world.

She located her rental, 'The Feisty One', and coughed a laugh. "Really? This is going to look professional." She climbed aboard, and made her way up to the open top bridge.

She dropped her bag and the cooler and immediately got out her phone. She texted the name of the ship to Mary, back in New York. Then she went below, using the key to open the main hatch. A quick survey told her everything was clean and in order.

Well, at least I have that going for me.

As she was loading up the little fridge with drinks Mary texted her back.

'Messaged relayed and big B confirmed.' Big B was what Mary was referring Paul Morgan as. Big Billionaire.

'The Feisty One? Is that name serious?' Mary sent.

Lydia texted back, 'Yup. Wish me luck.'

'I wish for you a big fat commission!' Mary returned.

Lydia could only laugh. It was okay for Mary to be excited about this potential deal. It was a little infectious, now that she thought about it. But she couldn't get too giddy. She needed to act professional.

Or at least pretend to.

She moved up to the bridge and started to check the equipment. After a short while someone called from below. "Hello, there!"

Lydia had to lean over to see who it was.

There was a man standing on the wharf, smiling up at her.

Oh, God. He's here! So soon!

Slightly flustered at being caught not fully prepared she said, "Yes! One moment!"

She leaned back, and quickly gave the bridge a visual once over.

He's here. This is happening. It really is happening!

She shook her head to clear her mind of Mary's gabbling voice, then climbed down the short ladder to the main deck.

She turned to look at him.

He was tall, muscular, and deeply tanned. His dark hair was short and cropped. He was wearing a simple pale blue buttoned collared shirt, and pale white cargo pants.

He grinned at her from behind his dark sunglasses. His teeth were bright to the point of being blinding.

"Hello," he said, again.

She was caught off guard. Sweet Lord, he was devastatingly handsome.

When she didn't respond immediately, the man hoisted an eyebrow at her in mild concern. "Oh, yes," he said. "I almost forgot." He removed his sunglasses and the picture was now complete.

Somewhere, deep inside her, Lydia felt her soul move.

Wow. Just... Wow.

Then, the man started to sing.

"The Rain In Spain Falls Mainly On The Plain." And as if this was the most normal thing to do, the man kept smiling at her.

Uh. What? Her mind managed to ask. Here she was in an island paradise being serenaded by a drop dead gorgeous billionaire. The very thought caused her head to spin.

When she didn't respond the man started to look a little worried, his expression one of slight alarm. It made him look endearing.

"The password. Wasn't that the password phrase we agreed on?" he asked.

"Password phrase?" Lydia asked.

"Yeah, so you know it is really me?"

Lydia suddenly felt like she was just smacked by Mary clear across from New York. "Right! Shoot! Sorry, I completely forgot!" And she had. How were you to know if this man really was the reclusive billionaire unless some sort of word or phrase were used. Mary had agreed to it before, but Lydia had forgot in the moment.

And looking at this Man-God up close, who could blame her.

"Permission to come aboard?" he asked. There was the tiniest hesitation, as if maybe he shouldn't board with this potentially crazy Realtor woman present.

"Yes," she said. "Please. Permission granted."

He stepped over the edge and onto the deck. Lydia tried not to ogle the muscular thighs that peaked out from under his shorts, and failed.

Once aboard, he offered his hand to her. "Hi, Paul Morgan," he said, making things more or less official.

Lydia shook his hand. "Lydia Jennings. Nice to finally meet you." At least she hoped that were the words spilling out of her mouth. She was still a little taken aback at how damn fine Paul Morgan looked.

And while shaking his hand she found she could only hold one thought in her head at that very moment: Thank God his name isn't Terry!

Chapter 3

Paul

Well, this trip is certainly off to a good start, Paul thought to himself while shaking Lydia's hand.

He found her stunningly attractive. Curves in all the right places, just the way he liked it. And she had a bright, beautiful smile.

But perhaps a little twitchy, he thought. Maybe it was just nerves. He was use to that. People usually got nervous or twitchy around him once they realize who he was. And how much he was worth.

He hoped she was more nerves than twitchiness.

But, boy, was she beautiful.

Once he realized he was still shaking her hand, he withdrew his, almost regretfully. He looked around.

"So, this is our ride?" he asked.

It appeared she took a moment to compose herself before answering. "Yup, reserved it yesterday after we got the call from your assistant. It was the best they had on such short notice." She looked apologetic.

Paul smiled at her, wanting to ease her mind. "No worries. Just as long as it doesn't sink it will do just fine."

They laughed together. Her laugh came easy and was pleasant on the ears.

"Would you like a drink, or snack? I was going to untie us so we could be off."

Paul held up his hands. "Actually, I can help with that. Allow me to handle the ropes."

And to her surprised expression, he hoped off the boat and back onto the dock. As he walked over to the first rope holding the boat to the dock, he glanced back at her. She was still standing in the same spot, looking more than a little amazed.

Yes, he thought, billionaires can untie ropes.

She seemed to snap out of her trance, smiled and quickly climbed up to the open bridge.

He watched her butt as she did this with interest.

Curves are underrated, he thought. And this woman has plenty of them.

As he uncoiled the thick rope from its mooring, he was hit with and sudden flash of Rebeca, his ex-girlfriend. She liked boats, too. So much so that she practically demanded he buy one for her. Like a smitten fool, he did, even though he didn't like it. Not only was it expensive, it hadn't been something he intended for her.

She was always demanding things. It hadn't started out that way. They had met at a friend's party, and she practically zeroed in on him from the moment he arrived. Like a heat seeking missile. Or a money seeking missile, as it turned out to be.

Once the mooring was untied he threw it into the back of the boat, then moved up to undo the front one. As he passed the bridge he glanced up at Lydia.

All he could see was her upper profile, and it did wonders for his mood. Lydia sort of reminded him of Rebeca. In a way.

Lydia noticed him looking and smiled. "Got that, okay?" she called out to him.

"Oh," he said, bringing his thoughts back to the task at hand. "Yeah, I got it." He undid the mooring, coiled it quickly and tossed it onto the boat.

Stop thinking about the one gold digger that got to you, he thought. There are more important things for your brain to be focused on right now. Like buying an island.

Once he was sure everything was fine, he came back to the middle of the boat and stepped over. Just then Lydia fired up the engines and the huge twin motors roared to life.

Paul quickly scampered up the step ladder to the bridge. Lydia had all the electronics turned on, and was concentrating on pulling the boat away from the pier. Other docked ships crowded around them, but Lydia seemed skilled enough to handle the situation.

Standing this close to her, he noticed how short she was compared to him. He was tall enough already. He found himself smiling. Short was good. Real good.

He found himself dawning his sunglasses, so she couldn't see where he was looking. He turned back, nonchalantly, and watched the dock, and all its ships, pull away from them.

If Rebeca was here, she would want him to buy all the ships in the bay. Or maybe the whole island nation. He frowned.

"Beautiful, isn't it?" Lydia asked. She was casting glances in his direction, but keeping her main attention to where she was going. Like a good captain should.

He gave her a big smile, his eyes taking her in completely from the safety of his sunglasses. She really was a sight to behold. "Yes," he said finally. "It is very beautiful." He found he was not talking about the island.

As if she didn't notice the intensity of his gaze she asked, "So, how long have you been looking?"

"Looking?" Was he that obvious? Staring at her?

"For an island? There aren't that many left to be had. I figured you must have been looking for a while."

"Oh," he said, turning so he was angled to see where they were headed. Vast blue ocean stretched out before them. He pondered his response. "Well, to be honest, I've been doing this for quite a long time."

"Looking for an island?"

"Buying them."

This took Lydia aback, and her eyebrows shot up from behind her sunglasses. She laughed. "Really? This isn't your first?"

"I have nine, currently."

"Nine islands! My God. That's more than some countries could say."

He found he was looking for an edge to her voice, something that indicated there was more to her comment than just genuine surprise. But he could find any.

Stop being such a suspicious jerk, he thought. Ever since he broke up with Rebeca he realized that the presence of other women, no, other people, made him slightly paranoid. He was starting to assume that because Rebeca wanted everything from him, then everyone wanted everything from him, too.

Lydia seemed to sense he was lost in thought. "Sorry, I didn't mean to blurt that out loud." She must of confused his silence with annoyance.

He hurried to ease her mind. "Not at all!" he said, with a laugh he hoped sounded as genuine as it was. "I find it kind of surprising, too, myself. It's not a common hobby." He grinned.

She laughed at this, and he was relieved to see he hadn't made her uncomfortable. Making her uncomfortable was the furthest thing he wanted to make her feel.

"No, I don't think it is. My sister, Mary, collects little crystal pigs. And those can get expensive. I can't quite get my mind around collecting anything that people and buildings could stand on."

Still smiling, Paul shrugged. "I love nature. I love the ocean. And more importantly, I love being away from cities. Islands seemed like the perfect idea."

"Resorts?" she asked.

"Pardon?" The motors were very loud, so he had to practically shout at each other.

"Are you going to build resorts on them? Like Yagenda has?"

"No, not at all. Each island I purchase gets assessed for its natural properties. Its flora and fauna. Then I have my lawyers work on getting them earmarked as nature preserves."

This seemed to take Lydia by surprise. Thankfully, her shocked expression quickly morphed into one of joy, complete with that incredible smile. "Really? That's amazing! So all your islands are nature preserves?"

"Nearly all of them. Some still need to go through the legal hoops. The idea is that as long as they are privately owned, then they will no longer be at risk for development. I want them left alone more or less."

Lydia was nodding in agreement, her smile growing wider. "Well, count me surprised. I thought because of the resort here, that you were interested in bringing it back up to snuff."

"Well, I might, but not for tourists, or any kind of profit making ventures. I was thinking the resort here could be converted into maybe a lab of some sort. For studying the island plant life and animals. Also, maybe the jumping off point for an oceanographic society." Saying the words out loud made him feel a tad sheepish. He was still with Rebeca when he started this silly idea, and had purchased his first two islands. When Rebeca realized his intent, she was almost furious with him.

Think of the money you could be making! She had practically screamed. Rich tourists love islands. And they are willing to pay big bucks to go sit on them. And you want to just... what? Do nothing with them?

He had stood resolute. It was something he felt passionately about, regardless of what she said. But she would have none of it.

If your going to waste them then at least let me have them, she had said. I could be turning a profit on each one within a year. Easy!

He had been aghast, and a little saddened at her attitude. Now she was demanding islands from him?

He had had enough and they broke up almost on the spot.

"A swanky lab for scientists and oceanographers?" Lydia said, bringing him back from his dark thoughts. "I like that idea. I really, really like that idea!" She was grinning from ear to ear, and looking directly at him, as if seeing him for the very first time.

Paul found he wanted to be in her gaze for a long time.

Suddenly, she pointed. "Hey, there it is. Yagenda Island!"

He turned to look. The profile of an island took up most of the horizon. From here, he could make out the lush jungle that seemed to encompass it entirely. One end, the south portion, had a higher elevation of hills than the north. A nearly unbroken line of white beach met the lapping blue waves of the ocean.

It was stunning.

"The resort is on the north side, in a bay. It will take us about twenty minutes to get there," she said.

"Take you time," he said. He was enjoying the view. He snuck a sideways glance in her direction. And not just of the island.

If she noticed his attention on her she didn't say anything. Instead, she pointed past them on the horizon, further out to sea.

"That looks to be the only other ship in the entire area. If you were looking for a place of isolation, this place certainly fits the bill."

He squinted at the distant ship, then cast his gaze all around them. Sure enough, there were no other boats at all.

Perfect.

Again, he found himself looking more at Lydia than the island jewel.

Who was this woman? What was her story? He found her really wanted answers to those questions. More than anything at that moment.

Whoa, easy buddy, he thought. A rebound situation would not be good right now. Not what you need. Just focus on the work at hand. Its the best thing for you.

But glancing at Lydia, he didn't think that thought process would hold for very long.

As they steered around the the island, toward the bay, Lydia took time to point out some features, and talk about the island's history. Paul took all this in, but only politely. He just liked hearing her talk. Watch her expressions, and the way she moved.

Soon, they entered the north bay. At its deepest point was a line of buildings, mostly resort rooms made to look like oversized huts. And above them, spread almost majestically was the main resort building. The Island Pearl Resort.

Lydia deftly manoeuvred them up to the only dock, which was covered in debris.

"I got this," Paul said, and scrambled down to the deck and grabbed the ships front rope. Once they were close enough, he hoped easily across to the dock, and he tied it to the moor. He then did the same to the rear one, as Lydia cut the engine.

No one came out to greet them. Nor were there any sounds, at least man made. They appeared to be completely alone.

Lydia jumped over onto the dock, clutching a bag stuffed with what looked to be Realtor related stuff.

As she landed, she slipped, and Paul quickly caught her in both arms.

"Are you okay?" he asked, enjoying this little movie moment.

"Yeah!" she said, laughing nervously as he let her go. "I'm just fine. Thank you." She seemed to appreciate his proximity more than he expected.

They turned to take in the island and the resort. Lush green jungle crowded in all around. Water lapped at the bay's white beach. The resort and all its buildings seemed to beckon to them.

It was quite amazing to look at, he thought. And again, his eyes were drawn to Lydia.

She seemed equally impressed with the island. "Wow. Quite the sight. So, any first impressions?"

He removed his sunglasses so she could see his eyes were firmly fixed onto hers. "My impression," he said, "is that I may have found more than I was expecting on this trip."

Chapter 4

Lydia

Did he just make a pass at me?

Lydia was stunned. She managed to blink out of her shock and return his smile. She guessed he was complimenting her, and she found that she liked it.

"I'm glad to hear it," she said for lack of a better response. What else do you say when a single, handsome billionaire tells you something like that?

Then, without thinking, she said, "I like to know that my clients are happy."

What the heck did I just say? She thought. She mentally scolded herself. Now he must think she was this eager to flirt with all her clients.

Paul seemed to sense her inner conflict, and said, "Well, I'm most certain that I may be the first client to truly mean it." Again, that easy smile. He turned toward the resort, and Lydia found herself breathing again.

"Shall we look around?" he asked.

"You bet," she said, glad the subject had changed. Keep it together girl! She fumbled out a folded laminated map of the resort. "You'll have to excuse me as I haven't the chance to be here before, so I can't go by memory."

"And here I was getting use to the idea that you were perfect," he said, grinning.

Oh, my God, he needs to stop that! She thought with alarm. But she found his flirtatious talk refreshing. And welcome. Terry almost never flirted with her. He was too lazy, and it wasn't in his programming to show any appreciation for a woman. Let alone her.

She chuckled and unfolded the map. From the dock, it was an easy walk through the first set of bungalows, and to the resort's front doors.

"Lead the way," he said. He had taken out his smart phone, which was a model she had never seen before, and was taking pictures.

They walked down the long dock, which was devoid of any features save for their own ship. The clomping of their feet on the old wood was the loudest sound. Just the rustling of the leaves in the trees and the occasional sound of water lapping against the dock was all that could be heard.

"Very peaceful," Paul said, as if reading her mind. "I like that there is no one here. No tourists, anyway."

"Yeah," she said in agreement. It was quite nice. Especially after almost an hour of the boat motors roaring in her ears. Without tourists, or staff, this place was a calm paradise.

I could live here, she found herself thinking. Maybe I could learn to be an Oceanographer, or study birds, or something. She glanced at Paul who was taking a picture of one of the bungalows. Maybe, if he bought this place, I could manage some type of position here.

The thought of the word position, and multiples, and the image of Paul's naked form pressed up against her suddenly flashed in her mind. It brought her up short. She found the thought very pleasant.

Paul noticed her stop suddenly. "Everything okay?" he asked. There was genuine concern in his voice.

Lydia found herself feeling flush, as if Paul could see what she had just imagined. "No, just fine, thank you," she managed. "Maybe just a little hot," she said. Hot because of him!

"I forgot to bring water," he said, and turned toward the boat. "I'll grab you a bottle."

"No that's okay. I have one here," she said. She quickly fished a plastic bottle of water out of her day bag and unscrewed the top. As she sipped she tried to get her mind back on track. Naked, sexy billionaires were nice to think about, but she had an island to sell.

Keep it together, and make this sale. Mary would kill her if she found out that her sister couldn't close a potential sale of this size because she allowed herself to become smitten with the client.

She envisioned Mary's look of disappointment, and it brought her back to reality.

She placed the bottle back into the bag. "Shall we continue," she asked.

Paul smiled and nodded. "Lead the way."

They walked off the docks and onto a cobblestone path that lead one way into the clutter of bungalows and the other direction up toward the resorts main building. Paul indicated the direction of the main complex and they sauntered up the path.

Various bungalows and service buildings lined their way, but everything was widely spaced. All of them were locked and the windows sealed to keep the elements from getting inside.

But it was quite obvious that nothing else had been done since, especially any upkeep.

Dirt, leaves and other debris cluttered the pathway. Paul playfully kicked aside a coconut out of their way.

"It looks like the insurance company didn't bother to spend any money for keeping things clean here," Paul said.

Lydia was relieved that he didn't say she, and her sister's company were responsible. "No, I guess not," she said, a little embarrassed. "After the original owners went belly up, the bank moved in. Afraid they would be stuck with something as large as an island and its resort they quickly sold to an insurance company, which for whatever reason, saw a way to turn a profit. But it looks like even they didn't want to spend any more than they had to."

"No security?" Paul asked.

Lydia shook her head, as she navigated around a small fallen tree that lay across the pathway. "None. Just a lot of locks and chains I guess."

"So there is no one else on the entire island?" He asked. "Except us two castaways?"

Again, Lydia felt the beginnings of a flush up her neck. "Not any more. The bank did, more out of necessity, I think. Once word got out the resort was closed they had some regular security guards. But once it changed hands to the insurance company, that ended. So, yes," she said, glancing at him almost shyly, "We are the only people on the entire island. Or should be, at least."

Paul was smiling. Almost mischievously. "I like the thought of that."

As Lydia was trying to interpret what that phrase could possibly mean, beyond the obvious, they came upon the resort building's front entrance. Huge double doors towered above them. Wrapped around the doors' pull handles, was a thick chain. At its center was a gigantic padlock. It was almost comical in size.

"Well, it doesn't look like anyone broke it," Lydia said, with a sense of professional relief. She would have had strong words with the insurance company if she had arrived to find the whole place ransacked.

"No doubt thieves were intimidated by this thing," Paul said, indicating the lock. "Got a key?" He smiled.

"You bet," she said, and fished out a ring of large keys. She had visited the insurance company's lawyers office before stopping to buy snacks, earlier. They had supplied her with the keys but not before asking if she would need a captain for the boat. That seemed to set the tone for the rest of the day.

As she looked through all the keys, in hopes of finding the correct one, she was suddenly struck with a thought. Paul did not say anything about her piloting the boat. He made no joke about her needing a captain. Unlike every other man she had encountered since her arrival, Paul did not make fun of her about it.

Interesting. More points for this guy. So far, he was racking them up.

She found the right key. It was huge, and even had the word 'Front' stencilled on its side. She slide the huge key into the equally huge lock, but found it wouldn't turn.

As she struggled with it, Paul pretended not to notice her plight and took pictures of the building.

She struggled to turn the key. After a few minutes of this nonsense, and on the verge of cursing and screaming, she looked to Paul. "Want to take a shot at this? I don't think its been opened in years."

"Sure thing," Paul said, and stepped forward. He took the key from her, almost gently, then gripped the lock.

Lydia was struck by his hands. They were large, and muscular. Almost like a carpenter's, or even a boxers. So this guy did more than sit behind a desk counting his money. He was in obviously good physical shape, and his hands more than completed the picture.

She found herself thinking what other body parts of his were in good working order, when Paul twisted the key, and the lock came undone.

"There we go," he said. "Just needed a special touch." That grin again.

Oh, it's on, she thought, and her heart started to hammer in excitement.

Before she could say anything, that could potentially betray her thoughts, Paul pulled the chains away from the door handles. Once cleared, he gripped both handles, then looked at her.

"Ready?" he asked.

"You bet," she said. She found she meant that in more ways than one.

He pulled on the doors, which opened outwards. With a loud squeeking protest, both doors swung open. A wide dimly lit foyer presented itself to them.

Paul piled the chain against the bottom corner of one of the doors, to prop it open.

For a moment Lydia had a sense of foreboding. As if they were about to enter a long abandoned haunted castle, as opposed to a neglected luxury resort.

"Big strong men first," she said to him with a grin.

Paul laughed at her comment. "Well, since there doesn't seem to be any around, I'll take the lead." He entered.

Trying not to think of all the other potential magical things those big strong hands could accomplish, she followed him inside.

Chapter 5

Lydia

As soon as they entered nothing jumped out to attack them, much to Lydia's relief.

The main entrance foyer was huge to the point of being cavernous. The vaulted ceiling extended up to the third story roof. Large, open entryways lead to the east and west, with what looked to be the start of the dining hall directly to the north.

A wide stairway, slowly curved along the wall leading up to vanish at the second floor. The floor was composed of wide square stone tile, and other than a fine layer of dust and sand, was none the worse for wear.

The entryway alone could easily have handled several dozen arriving tourists at the same time and still had room for a football team to play a game.

"Wow," Paul said, stating the obvious.

"Yeah, wow is right," Lydia agreed.

They both stood for a few moments drinking in this huge wide structure. And this was but a fraction of what the main building had to offer.

"Doesn't look to bad for being ignore for several years," he said, kicking at the dusty floor.

"Guess they had it sealed up pretty good," Lydia said. "The construction used the best materials and most advanced architectural techniques. Or so the brief says."

Just looking at it all one could tell a tremendous effort was made to make this one of the finest buildings in all the South Pacific. To think some greedy idiots ruined it was almost an offence on common sense.

"Doesn't look like we even need flashlights," Paul said.

Lydia agreed. Most of the windows had some amount of outside boarding done to them, but enough space was left that the bright early sunshine found its way in. That and the wide bright colored walls helped bounce light around.

"I have a couple of flashlights, just in case," she said.

"For someone who had to show up in a rush, you came prepared."

Again, a compliment. She smiled. She was getting use to them.

But she didn't want him to stop.

"Let's just take a peak in the dining hall, then head upstairs and work our way down," he said.

Lydia nodded and they walked across the huge room, their footsteps echoing off the walls. Other than the occasional breeze from the front entrance, it was otherwise as silent as a tomb.

They stood in the double wide entryway of the dining hall. There was no longer any furniture. Anything of worth had long since been stripped away to sell. So all that was here were some discarded folding chairs and tables leaning up against one wall. The rest of the huge hall was barren of features. At the far end was a stage, long unused.

Lydia could almost imagine this hall full of people and wide, round tables. Food of all kinds being served to happy couples, and newly weds. A cheerful band could have played on the stage, taking requests and keeping the mood upbeat throughout the meal.

Now it just looked sad. Like the rest of the complex.

The Realtor in the back of her mind waved a red flag and Lydia glanced over at Paul. He seemed lost in thought as his eyes took in the vast space.

"I think with a couple of throw pillows and a little dusting, this place would be as good as new," she said with some levity.

For a brief moment, Paul did not appear to comprehend her dry quip, but then he burst into laughter. Slightly relieved, Lydia found herself laughing, too.

"Actually," Paul said, "I was thinking this would convert well into a bowling alley."

Lydia couldn't read is dead pan expression, but when he laughed again, she joined in.

And a sense of humor, too, she thought. This keeps getting better by the minute.

"Come on," he said. "Let's check upstairs."

They went back into the main foyer then started to ascend the stairs along the wall. It was so wide that a half dozen tourists hauling luggage could have climbed these steps and not got in each other's way. The banisters looked to be of a thick mahogany and just underlined how much money was used here.

"I can imagine children sliding down those and causing their parents to have heart attacks," Paul said, indicating the banisters.

"Yeah," Lydia said. Then she found herself blurting, "Do you have any children?" And immediately regretted it.

Paul's face transformed from one of outgoing happiness, to a sudden sullen gloom. "No," he answered. "I don't." And went quiet, instead focusing on the steps they were climbing.

Ah, damn! Lydia thought. What did she just do? Based on her research of Paul, she never considered looking into the public details of his personal life. She sensed that asking such a question just made whatever friendly progress they had going slip into reverse.

Then, unexpectedly, Paul looked over to her and said, "Well, not yet, anyway." And offered her a wide, glowing smile.

Lydia's heart was suddenly hammering in her chest. Whoa.

The reached the second floor entryway, while the stairs continued up to the third, and final floor. Directly across was another wide hall, with vaulted ceilings. It appeared to some sort of resting area. On its far side were some double glass doors, that lead out to a huge balcony.

They looked down the east wing, then west wing hallways. Dozens of room doors presented themselves.

"What do you think? Should we check out the balcony?" he asked. She was a little relieved that whatever mood swing she accidentally triggered had gone. He appeared back to his old, cheerful self.

"Sure," she said. As they approached, she noticed another set of chains, and a padlock, but this one was considerably smaller than the one at the front.

"You are the key master," Paul said.

She fished out the key ring again, and started to hunt through them. No kids, huh? She thought. Which meant several possibilities. He didn't want kids. He couldn't have kids. Or he just hadn't found someone to procreate with. Yet.

Finding the key she inserted it into the padlock. Thankfully, it did not fight back and unlocked. As she unwrapped its small chain from the doorhandles she looked to Paul who was trying to peer through the boards to see outside.

At his handsome profile she was struck with a thought. This guy is most definitely procreation worthy. And then some.

"There we go," she said. She stepped back as Paul pushed the wide doors outward.

They were hit with bright sunshine and a warm breeze, as they emerged from the the grey murk of the resort's interior.

Like the rest of the building, the balcony was gigantic. No doubt it was used for an eating area as well.

As they stepped out, Lydia's phone burred, indicating a message.

"Oh," she said. "This will just take a moment."

"No problem, take your time," Paul said, and walked toward the edge of the balcony.

The text message was from Mary. It read, "Handsome? Gorgeous? Studly? Tell me!" Lydia could practically hear her sister's voice hollering these words from New York, demanding answers.

"Oh, boy," she said. She didn't have time for this right now. She simply texted back, 'Busy now. Later.'

She hoped that would placate Mary. At least for the moment.

Lydia walked over to join Paul at the edge of the balcony.

"Stunning, huh?" he asked.

It was. The view was absolutely spectacular. At this height, they had a commanding view of almost the entire bay, save for some overgrown trees which muddled it a bit. But the vista was breath taking, to say the least. Deep green jungle, aqua marine ocean, bright blue endless sky.

Lydia needed a moment to truly appreciate what she was seeing. "Sheesh," she said, finally.

Paul was equally impressed. "I guess this explains the price, eh?" he said, indicating all before them.

Lydia laughed. "Definitely. And worth every penny." She said this with the widest smile possible, showing as much of her pearly whites as she could.

Paul laughed. "I guess I asked for that. But, still, I've been to many places in the world, and I am completely bowled over by this."

Lydia's inner Realtor was now screaming at her, with trumpets blaring. He's sold on the place! Get him to agree to a price while he's weak with the appreciation of its beauty! Go! Go!

"Well, this is quite unique, you must admit," she started to say, slipping into business mode. That was why they were there, after all. "Perhaps if you looked at this agreement, I'm sure you'll find - "

Just then her phone rang loudly in her bag.

"Ah, crud," she said. Bad moment or what? "Let me just get rid of them."

"Sure," Paul said, but instead of taking the agreement from her hand he returned his gaze back to the view.

Damn it! She thought. Moment ruined!

She snatched the still ringing phone from her bag and checked the display. It was from Mary.

"One second," she said to Paul, but he didn't seem to hear her, lost in the majestic view.

Lydia took a few steps away, then answered. "You have some very bad timing, sister mine!" she hissed into the phone.

From clear across the planet, her sister responded with, "Why? Are you two naked already? Sealing the deal, as it were?"

"No, but I was close," Lydia said, trying not to growl. "I have him on the ropes. He's in love with place. I just have to get it down on paper."

"Ropes? Love? Getting down? Sister, you just can't keep your hands off our clients can you?"

Lydia made an effort to count to five before speaking. "Look, things are going well. I should have a tentative agreement soon. If you would just leave me alone to - "

"But that is just my way!" Mary interrupted. "You know how darn paranoid I am. When I didn't hear from you I started to worry. Thought I'd call the navy, or the marines, or whatever it is they have down there. What do they have, anyway?"

Lydia had to set her sister straight once and for all, or this could very well go on all day. Well, at least until the agreement was signed, then Mary can pester her all she wanted.

"I want you to listen to me, please," Lydia said.

"Okay, little sister, I'm listening," Mary said. Lydia sensed she was still not being serious.

"Listen carefully," Lydia continued. "It is very, very important that you - ."

Her phone connection suddenly went dead with an audible click.

Having lost her momentum, Lydia gaped at the phone's display, trying not to curse. No signal.

"Shoot," she said, glaring at the little screen.

"What's up," Paul asked, walking over to her.

"Ah, my signal cut out. Dropped the call on me."

"No worries," he said. "Here, you can use mine." He produced a sleek black phone that looked like it belonged on the set of a science fiction movie. "Its a prototype from one of my companies. The military uses it and will never lose its signal."

"Ever?" Lydia asked, impressed.

"Ever," he said. "Well, unless someone shoots the satellite out of the - ." He stopped talking, staring at the screen.

"What is it?" Lydia said.

"Well, that's odd." He looked at the phone, concerned. "There is no signal. But that's impossible."

"We both lost our signal? Huh," she said. "Maybe someone did shoot the satellite out of the sky after all."

Paul was not sharing the joke. He wasn't smiling. He looked worried.

Uh oh, Lydia thought, alarm bells starting to ring in her head.

"The only other way," Paul said, thinking out loud, "was if the signal was being purposely jammed." He looked up from the phone to her. His face serious. "Maybe we should just return to the boat and - ." He glanced out toward the bay, and froze. His eyes widened.

Lydia looked.

Through the leaves and branches of the over grown trees they could see the bay almost clearly. At the end of the dock sat their boat. But behind it was another ship. A large one. It looked like it had just arrived because men were jumping off of it and hurrying down the dock.

But there was one particular detail that had her immediate and full attention:

All the men were carrying guns.

Chapter 6

Oswald

Oswald was extremely pleased with himself, although he made an effort to hide that fact from his men. No need to give them reason to get sloppy.

Almost on schedule, they spotted Morgan's boat appearing on the horizon. This had given credence to Oswald's decision to pay the Tarangian Harbor Master almost double what he originally intended. That decision had paid off. With that information they knew exactly when Morgan would arrive.

And arrive he did.

Despite Reeka's murmuring protests, Oswald made sure no one moved from their position, or even started the engines, for fear that anything at all might raise Morgan's suspicions. Having your prey escape because someone was impatient would not be ideal. In fact, given his current crew of thugs, it would be quite fatal.

Once Morgan's boat had vanished into Yagenda's cove, he gave the signal. All pieces were now in play.

As they had approached the island and full speed, Oswald cycled through all their communications one final time. When everyone checked in, only then did he tell Kenneth to activate the electronics jammer.

The device was as ingenious as it was an annoyance. Not only would it kill any electronic signals, especially from satellites, it greatly limited his own communications with his men. Kenneth had attuned things so that, at the very least, they could use short range walkie talkies. But even then they would be almost unreliable.

No matter. Everyone knew the plan, and everyone was well versed on its contingencies if anything went awry. Not that it would. There was only a fat cat billionaire, and some Realtor to contend with. He expected things to go smoothly.

He found himself grinning as his ship pulled into the bay, presenting a full view of the resort. But his own eyes locked on Morgan's rental boat, firmly tied to its moors on the dock.

Perfect.

As Reeka pulled their own ship up behind Morgan's, the Filipino mercenary barked orders to the men who jostled along the ships railings to be the first on the docks; to be the first to nab Morgan.

Oswald had offered a bonus to whomever tagged the billionaire. Everyone were also very much aware that he was needed alive. So, special precautions had been taken.

They would hunt, but not kill. But if anyone got in their way, then that would be a problem easily solved.

With a thump, the ship hit the dock, and men leapt off with a shout, or cheer. Oswald could not blame them. This was an easy job, and stealth was no longer a necessity once they had made landfall.

"Secure the moorings," Oswald shouted. "Check their boat." It was all unnecessary, but he wanted to remind everyone who was in charge.

As men hurried about, most heading toward the resort, Oswald scanned the buildings. Morgan was here, somewhere. Perhaps hidden like an egg in an easter egg hunt.

A billion dollar egg.

His eyes settled on the massive resort building that dominated the hillside above the bay. He had study its layout, along with the entire complex the night before. There was little in the way of hiding places, if that was how Paul Morgan wanted to play it.

As Oswald descended from the bridge to the deck, one of his men approached.

"Their boat is clear. Nothing there."

"No phones, or devices?"

"No, sir."

"Okay. Check the fuel, and prepare the boat. We'll be taking it with us."

"Yes, sir," the man said, and hurried off to do as ordered.

Originally they were going to just leave the rental, but since they were pirates and kidnappers he figured why not. Even though soon enough he would be able to buy hundreds just like it, he enjoyed the idea of just taking it, because he could.

Oswald stepped of the deck and onto the dock, Reeka following behind. He could sense the shorter man's tension.

"How long do you think?" Reeka asked. It was his subtle way of needling at Oswald. Keep the boss on his toes.

Oswald made a show of thinking about the question, then said, "Twenty minutes, and Morgan will be secured, and we'll be pulling out to sea."

Reeka chortled. "Twenty minutes? Then twenty dollars says longer. Maybe much longer."

Oswald frowned, but agreed. "Fine. You're on."

Reeka grinned, then hurried off to supervise the men. He was always a glass half empty type of personality, but if Oswald was honest with himself, that was exactly why he liked having him around on jobs such as these. To keep Oswald on his toes. To try and expect the unexpected.

And in twenty minutes he would know if Reeka was right.

Chapter 7

Lydia

Both Lydia and Paul gaped down at the armed men now swarming up the dock, and vanishing into the small warren of the resort buildings.

One heartbeat. Then two.

Paul was the first to break out of his shock and said, "This would be a great time to tell me that those are security guards who work for the insurance company."

It took a moment longer for Lydia to respond. "Nope," she said, still staring at the scene below. "Not at all."

In the distance, she could see a pair of men now standing on the dock beside the new ship. Could it be the ones in charge? Who the hell were they?

There have only been a few instances in Lydia's life where she encountered mind numbing fear. Nearly all were the result of a near accident of some sort, like when she lost control of her car in a snow storm and skidded off the highway into a snow bank. Fortunately, she and Mary, who was with her at the time, were not hurt. But the whole thing terrified her right down to her very core.

This was a different type of fear, a more sinister cousin. This time, it was other people that were creating the sensation. She'd never felt anything like it. It looked like these men might be here to kill them.

She stood frozen on the spot. Her mind locked up. Oh, my God. I'm going to die! Her mind screamed at her.

It was Paul who managed to snap her out of it. "We should go. Now." He had firmly, but gently, put a hand on her shoulder and was now guiding her toward the balcony doors. She moved, but almost as if she were in a trance, pushed along by the will of someone else. Her own will locked away in a tiny room in the back of her mind, safe.

"I... I don't..." she stammered for no reason. What was she trying to say?

"It's okay," Paul said, and his tone seemed to convey that he meant it. "Let's head out the back. Quickly." And with that, he kept pushing her along toward the huge stairs.

She found herself turning her head to stare at him. Why couldn't she think?

Guns. Men with guns.

As they crested the stairs and began their descent, Paul slipped his hand off her shoulder to take a grip of her arm at the elbow. His focus was entirely on the stairwell, but he looked incredibly serene.

For her benefit? He was being cool so as to keep her calm?

What a nice guy, she thought, then frowned. Given the circumstances she needed to think of other, more urgent matters.

Paul stopped them almost immediately upon descending the stairs. He crouched down, so as to look through the banister, and down into the foyer below.

"We should hurry - ," she began to say, then stopped as she heard them. Voices. Right outside.

From Paul's vantage point he was peering directly at the open doorway below. He was making a huge effort not to be seen, as Lydia could see only a sliver of sunlight from the door on one side of his face.

The voices again. This time louder. Much louder.

Then, the hard slapping of shoes on the tiled floor below. A huge shadow bounced against the one wall across from her.

Someone was inside.

Paul's eyes widened fractionally as he looked at who was there. Without looking directly at Lydia he placed a finger against his lips. Quiet.

As if she needed to be reminded. Then again, given her state of mind, maybe she did. Her senses were that of a base animal, who wondered into a cave only to have a predator arrive to block the entrance.

More slapping of shoes. Someone else arrived, more shadows. This time voices spoke to each other, loud and echoey in the cavernous foyer.

Men, speaking in a language she didn't understand. But their meaning was clear, and urgent. They were looking for something.

Or someone.

Paul now eased back from the banister, and when satisfied he was not spotted looked at Lydia. He nodded his head, indicating they should go back up.

Again, he guided her by the arm. But now her mind seemed to be returning to her. Thoughts rushed in that had previously been held at bay by fear. Why was this happening? What did they want? What were they going to do?

They reentered the second floor hallway, but this time, instead of the balcony, Paul moved them down the west wing hallway at a hurried pace. They weren't running, the noise would carry, but the two of them were certainly hustling along.

"Where are we going?" Lydia managed to whisper after a few moments. Paul's eyes bounced from hotel room door to door.

"A place to hide," he said. His tone was very casual, without tension. As if this sort of conversation was an everyday occurrence. "They will have to search each room. So if he get far enough away, it may buy us some time." He kept passing each closed door, not pausing at any of them.

"Buy us time for what?" she asked hopefully.

He spared a moment to glance at her. Arching a brow he said matter of factly, "To run away."

Lydia almost laughed. Oh, God. Was she getting hysterical? No, just caught up in the moment, and almost bewildered by his serene presence.

Paul craned his neck, looking further down the hall. "There." He pointed.

At the end of the hall was the fire escape door. Lydia thought she had never seen something so welcome.

"Come on," Paul whispered, but as he did, there was a shout from behind them.

Without stopping, they both looked behind them.

No one was racing after them, guns blazing, thankfully. But from this angle Lydia could see shadows playing along the top of the foyer wall. Someone was on the stairs. They would see them any second.

Lydia and Paul came up on the fire escape door, only to see yet another chain wrapped around its push handles, with yet another padlock.

Without slowing, Paul steered them toward the final door on the right. It had a faded sign on it that read 'House Keeping'.

He pressed them up against the door and turned the knob. It wasn't locked. Then he pushed it open an inch. It was silent. Then, with another shout behind them, he opened the door a little wider and they both slipped inside.

As Paul quietly closed the door behind them, Lydia took in their new surroundings. It was nothing more than a very tiny utility closet. There had been some wooden shelving, but most had been removed, or was piled up in one corner. There was an empty light socket above them in the high ceiling amongst a canopy of spiderwebs.

There was other discarded junk pushed up against the walls. Along the top of one wall was a thin window, just above eye level. One glance told her that neither she or Paul would ever fit through it.

There was nothing here of use. Nothing that could save them.

Her eyes completed their circuitous route of the little room, and then settled them on Paul.

He was breathing a little heavy, a slight sheen of perspiration on his forehead. But he did not looked panicked in the least.

And he was looking at her.

"Are you okay?" He whispered.

His concern, despite their terrifying circumstances touched her, and for the smallest of moments she felt tears welling up.

"I think so, yeah. Thanks for asking." Her hushed tone had a slight hitch in it.

Do not cry, girl. If that brought the men with guns down on them now then that would truly suck.

Paul's expression of concern eased and he stepped closer to her. Not that he had far to go. He gently held her shoulders.

"We are going to be fine. Trust me." He said. And for whatever reason, she did no doubt it. What was it about this guy, anyway?

She suddenly realized her heart was pounding up in her throat. Was that from fear, or from something else?

"Did you see it?" he asked.

"See what?" she said, genuinely dumbfounded by the question.

"The padlock on the door."

"Oh. Yes, I did."

"Think you can find the key that opens it?"

Her heart ramped up its assault on her chest cavity. Unlocking that padlock would get them out of here. They wouldn't be trapped. The thought made her almost giddy.

"I think so, if its marked." She realized she still had her day bagged clutched to her side. She hadn't given it a single thought since seeing the men on the pier. Relieved, she reached in and pulled out the large key ring.

Unbidden, the keys clinked loudly in her hand.

And at that very moment, from directly outside their door, a voice shouted.

Chapter 8

Paul

Someone had found them.

Paul put his hands up and placed them firmly on the door. Maybe he could slow them down? Let Lydia escape. He could try and pull the man inside the room when he entered, let Lydia get past them. Or he could jump out now, and try and take the man down.

Paul's heart was now pounding hard. His adrenaline had shot up his senses, every detail around him crisp and heightened.

Another shout, from the same position outside the door. But this time they heard someone push at the fire escape handles, which only rattle with movement, the chains and lock keeping it securely closed.

They don't know we are here, Paul thought. Yet.

Glancing around, he found a narrow piece of shelving against the wall next to his leg. He grabbed it, being careful not to make any noise. He motioned Lydia to move back, not that there really was anywhere she could go. Holding the shelving up in one hand, he grasped the door handle.

If the person outside intended on coming in here, Paul was going to surprise them. The turning of the door handle would give him barely a second to react, pull open the door and try and brain the other guy.

Good plan, Paul, he thought. Your flimsy piece of wood against a lunatic with a machine gun. This will end well.

Paul pushed aside those negative thoughts. He stayed focused on the door handle, ready for it to move.

He sensed Lydia next to him, in the cramped space. Thankfully, despite the initial shock of the situation, she had settled down. Now she seemed almost like she was ready to fight, too.

Then, from somewhere deeper in the building came another voice.

The person outside cursed, or at least it sounded like it could be, all angry. Then he heard the man move back down the hall streaming more angry words.

After a few moments, the man's voice faded away, moving off to another part of the complex.

Paul counted to ten. Then he released the handle and lowered the shelving. Both he and Lydia exhaled.

Lydia was blinking hard, obviously relieved.

"That was close," Paul said. He glanced up at the window, only to see how disappointingly small it was.

"Did you understand what he was saying?" Lydia said.

Paul gave a small shrug. "Not really. I recognize it as Tagalog. He's Filipino. But as to what he was saying I have no idea."

"He sounded mad. Like real mad." Lydia said, casting a concerned look at the door, as if it might burst open suddenly with an angry Filipino arriving to prove her right.

"He didn't find what he was looking for. Not yet at least," he said.

"Us?"

"Me," he said, and frowned. "They're here for me. The rich guy. Has to be. This can't be just a random encounter. Not here. Not now."

Lydia considered this. "Wow. That really, really sucks."

Paul nodded in agreement. But they didn't have time to think on the men's motives, for which Paul was certain of anyways. They needed to figure out what to do.

"So, now what?" Lydia said, as if reading his thoughts.

He considered, chewing on his lower lip. "Well, I don't think hiding in here is an option."

"I don't know," Lydia said, giving the tiny room a look over. "It has a rustic feel to it. Real homey."

Paul shook his head. "It's only a matter of time before they do a proper search of the complex. Go from room to room. Floor to floor."

"That is a lot of rooms. The main complex has several hundred, including the two basements."

"Which is a good thing, it will buy us some extra time. I think the smart move is to just get as far away from here as possible. Like to the other side of the island, maybe."

"Can't get far on an island."

"Yes, but I prefer my odds out there, than in here," he said, looking meaningfully at the door. "Where ever we hide in here, we'll be boxed in. Not ideal."

As if struck with a thought, Lydia pulled out her cell phone and checked it. Paul did the same.

His screen was active, but the signal was dead. Considering the cost of this model that should not happen at all.

"Still no signal," Lydia said.

"They are blocking us. This just makes me think that this was planned. They knew I was coming here. I just don't know how."

Lydia visibly blanched. "It was not me. I swear on a stack of bibles that I had nothing -"

Paul held up his hand to stop her, and grinned. "I know that. Don't worry. But there had to be another angle, something they managed to exploit."

He shrugged. "It could have been anything, really. But this is a line of thought that won't help us now. We need to be moving."

Lydia looked down at the keys in her hand. Quickly, she went through them. She held up a group of a half dozen keys. "One of these might be it."

"Might be?"

"Yeah. None are marked fire escape, second level. They are just small padlock keys."

"You have to go through each, one by one?"

"Yup."

"And unwrap the chain?"

"Yup."

"And open the old creaky fire escape door?"

"Yup."

"Without being seen or heard the entire time?"

"Yup."

Paul grinned. "Sounds like a plan, captain."

Lydia stifled a laugh. Which Paul thought was a good sign. At least she was no longer in a state of shock.

"Okay, then. Ready?" Paul said as he gripped the door handle again.

"Ready," she said. "Oh, wait!"

Paul had started to turn the handled and stopped in alarm. "What?"

"Once were are outside where do we go?"

Paul took a second to consider, then said, "Anywhere they're not."

Lydia nodded. "Okay. I like your plan."

Paul turned the handle the rest of the way, then pried the door open a sliver. Holding his breathe, he peeked out.

There wasn't an angry Filipino, waving a machine gun, waiting to pounce on them.

He opened the door a fraction more, then eased out a little and peered down the hall.

It was completely empty, all the way to the far east end. No one was there. Which didn't mean anything. They could already be searching the rooms on this level. Paul wouldn't know until they stepped out into the hallway. Then it would be to late.

"Anything?" Lydia whispered from beside him.

"No. All clear," he said, and took a step out into the hall.

It was very quiet, eerily so. Maybe the men had moved off to another location to search. It didn't matter. He and Lydia had to leave. But going back down the hall, and down the stairs to the front entrance was to crazy to contemplate.

"Okay," he said. "Give it a try."

Lydia moved out of the hall, glancing briefly toward the stairs. Then she stood in front of the fire escape door and gripped the padlock. She already had a key in her grip and tried it.

Paul kept watch, keeping himself directly behind her, so if anyone started shooting, they would hit him instead of her.

Lydia mumbled a curse when the key didn't work. She tried another.

Paul's mind was racing. Was this a planned attack? How the heck could they have known he was coming here, if he didn't even think of it until a couple of days earlier?

He had previously hired a security firm to handle all his travelling, but over the years it just seemed more of a hindrance than a necessity. If you were a rich target, what better indication than having some bodyguards shadowing your every move?

No, he changed his mind. Hiding in plain sight felt better. At least then he could blend into a crowd, or move about without drawing attention to himself.

But now, he didn't seem to sure. Perhaps, this could have been avoided if he had kept the body guards. He recalled the number of men outside and their fierce armaments. Well, a lot of body guards. And a tank.

Lydia cursed again. "They didn't work. Should I keep trying?"

"Yeah, keep at it. No point hiding again." He tried to sound sure of himself, but if he was being honest, he had no idea if this course of action was the right one. How could he know? How could anyone?

Well, other than maybe bodyguards.

Lydia started to try another set of keys. He was impressed with how she had recovered from her initial shock. Now she was just as bound and determined to get out of here as he was. Cowering in a corner wasn't going to solve anything.

He was then struck with a morbid thought. The men were here for him, that was for certain. But they weren't here for Lydia. She was just a bystander. Someone that got in the way. And if they let her live, a potential witness.

Paul frowned at this. For all intents and purposes Lydia would be seen as a liability. Disposable.

No, he thought. He wasn't going to let it get to that point. She would not be harmed. He wouldn't let it. No matter what that cost him - whether that be money or his life.

There came a sound from what Paul thought was the direction of the stairway. Shouting?

"Got it!" Lydia said, joy obvious in her voice.

More voices from the foyer now, he was certain of it. A large group was here now.

He didn't mention the voices, and instead said, "Okay, lets get this chain off." Against his will, he turned his back to the hallway and the growing shouts and tried to help Lydia unwrap the chains from the door handles.

It was a tangled mess. Paul started sweating, hands fumbling about.

"Let me," Lydia said, pushing him aside. She quickly managed the little puzzle of the wrapped chain, and it started to unravel.

Paul bent down to catch the chain, so it didn't clatter to the floor.

More voices. He couldn't tell if they were closer or not. He felt he might be starting to panic. They would be seen at any moment.

Finally, the chain gave way, and the door handles were clear. Paul eased the chain into a little pile on the floor. Lydia had put her hand on the push handle. She swallowed once, then gently pushed at it.

For whatever reason, the door suddenly popped open with a loud squawk!

Paul and Lydia cursed in unison.

More voices from behind them. They had to have heard the door.

"Go!" he hissed, not looking back.

Lydia moved quickly out the open fire escape door with Paul right behind her.

Chapter 9

Lydia

They were outside.

Lydia's heart had returned to her throat, pounding away at an insane speed. She looked around.

The fire escape they stood on was old, and its metal was rusted. Steep stairs went up to the third floor, while the stairs also descended down to the ground level. Below, through its metal grating, she could see a small concrete landing next to another door. Bushes and trees cluttered up against the building's wall, as if the jungle was trying to claim the resort for itself.

Directly across from them was the jungle canopy, thick and green, and seemingly impenetrable. Below and to the north she could make out the rooftops of bungalows and other buildings.

Thankfully, there was no one else around.

"I think they may have seen us," Paul said, from beside her. He still held the piece of shelving, but this time he was trying to wedge it in between the doorhandles. "This might slow them."

"What now?" Lydia asked, and felt foolish. She knew what now, but wanted him to tell her.

"Get to the ground," he said, finally jamming the wood into place. "Hurry." He was still speaking in hushed tones. Someone outside might hear them.

She moved to the narrow stairs. Fear still gripped her, as her movements were stilted and almost robotic. She started to descend, gripping the railing for support. She didn't want to pitch forward or over the side.

The metal of the fire escape rattled and creaked. It seemed secure, but just old and neglected. The stairs were a single long flight down the side of the wall to the ground, and every step she took caused the stairs to wobble more.

She looked back to see Paul had only descended a couple of stairs. He was looking at the door.

"Come on," she hissed. What was he doing? Did he have it in his mind to try and stop whoever might come through the door? No, she thought. He was thinking of just slowing them down to give her time to escape.

"Don't!" she said. "Let's go!" she said.

Paul looked from the door to her. Whatever crazy plan he had he must of decided against it. He kept climbing down the stairs toward her.

Relieved, Lydia climbed down the rest of the creaky stairs. At the bottom, her feet touched solid concrete. She crouched down, and leaned against the wall. There was another fire escape door here, identical to the one above. She doubted anyone would come through it as it, too, would be chained and padlocked from the other side.

Thick, high bushes and small trees crowded up against the wall here, providing ample cover for her to hide. When she tried to listen all she could here was the noise of the jungle itself, and the creaking of the fire escape as Paul descended.

In moments, he was crouching down beside her.

"What were you doing up there?" she asked.

Paul offered a small shrug. "Thought I could surprise them, or something. Buy you time to get away."

"Not a good idea," she said and tried to look annoyed. But really, she felt touched at his gesture. She felt some relief that he was looking out for her, and not running off on his own and abandoning her. He certainly wasn't that kind of person, she knew.

She said, "Okay, now where - ".

Someone crashed against the door above them. It appeared the wood in the handles held firm. For the moment.

Paul grabbed her hand. "Gotta move," he said, and they were off.

Still crouching they hurried north along the wall, keeping low. The bushes and trees were tall here and kept them hidden from view.

As they approached the corner of the building Paul stopped. Behind them, the fire escape door rattle violently. Someone was kicking or pushing against it. The next one would let them through.

Paul glanced around the corner of the building. Lydia turned to look back up at the fire escape, but was suddenly pulled along again by Paul.

The fire escape door exploded open. Lydia caught a quick glance of a man stepping onto the fire escape, and then her view was obscured by the corner of the building. Paul was taking them along at an angle so they would not be seen.

At the back of the resort building was a huge, wide balcony that stretched across almost half its width. Debris and leaves covered every inch.

Paul kept them to the edge of it, not daring to cross as it was a wide open space. Instead, he was leading them toward a cluster of bungalows a short distance ahead.

Lydia's head was swivelling around, trying to see if they had been spotted. The rushing of the wind in her ears, and the rattling of leaves at their feet, kept her from getting a clear idea if anyone was near them.

As they entered the space between two bungalows, Lydia looked back. She gasped.

A man was now standing at the corner of the building, exactly where they had been moments before. And he was looking right at her. Then she moved out of view.

"He saw us!" she said.

"Keep going," Paul said. They were moving along the side of a bungalow. "We'll try and lose him in the jungle."

It sounded like a good plan to Lydia's panicked mind. Of course, it was their only plan.

Paul checked around the corner of the bungalow, glancing in both directions. Lydia could feel the other man approaching them from behind. He would be there in seconds.

Then they saw the last of the buildings, and the jungle beyond. Once there, she was certain they would be safer.

Suddenly, from behind she heard a shout. She turned her head, still running.

The man was behind them now, pistol in hand. He was very close, and at a full run. He was getting closer. There was no time to get into the jungle.

They weren't going to make it.

Chapter 10

Lydia

"He's here!" Lydia said.

Paul turned to look, his eyes widening at the sight of the other man so close to them. They had seconds before he was upon them.

"Here!" Paul said, and altered their course to run around the corner of a bungalow.

But instead of continuing on, Paul stopped and turned.

"Stay back," he said, the tension in his voice was palpable. He pushed her back away from him. He crouched at the corner of the building, like a football player about to tackle someone.

"What are you - ", she started to say when she gasped in surprise.

The other man ran around the corner at that exact moment. He hadn't altered his speed and was running flat out. His eyes widened in surprise at finding them right there in front of him.

Then Paul jumped at him.

With a loud grunt Paul connected before the man could react to the new situation. Both men tumbled to the ground.

Something landed beside Lydia. Not wanting to look away from the Paul and the man now wrestling on the ground, she found herself looking to see what it was.

It was a pistol. The man must of dropped it when Paul connected with him.

Lydia blinked at it then over at the men.

Paul was larger than the other man, but that didn't stop his opponent from putting up one heck of a fight. They grappled in the dirt, Paul trying to keep him pinned.

For several moments Lydia watched transfixed, unable to move.

Paul now had the other man pinned to the ground beneath him, but didn't seem sure what to do with him. Then Paul punched him once in the face.

The other man grunted in pain, but was not knocked out. It just seemed to annoy him.

Oh, God, Lydia thought. What could she do? Jumping into the fray didn't seem to be the best idea. She wasn't any kind of fighter herself. Kick him, maybe?

Just then, the man got an arm free and punched Paul across the jaw. Paul's head snapped back and caused him to tumble off the man.

Oh, no! She thought.

Both Paul and the man stood, eyeing the other wearily.

The other man was definitely smaller than Paul, but wiry. He was Filipino, and wore dark trousers and a black shirt, which was now torn at one sleeve.

Paul seemed to have recovered and started to step toward the other man, his fists raised up, ready for more.

Then, the other man suddenly produced a small knife from his pocket.

Paul froze.

The Filipino grinned. He was missing some front teeth, and what was left was stained a deep yellow.

"To bad I can't kill you," the man said. His voice was high pitched, almost squeaky. "But I can still cut you good. Sell you piece by piece."

Paul looked grimly at the knife but he didn't back away. "Not today, you're not," he replied.

Lydia was certain that it was pure bravado on Paul's part. She had a partial awareness of her research of him, and disarming thugs in a tropical setting was not in his skill set.

The little man was enjoying the moment. The knife gave him all the advantage he needed now, regardless of Paul's size.

"Gonna carve my name in you," the man said, still grinning. "Then I'm gonna have a go at your stupid woman."

Lydia felt anger flare in her chest like a torch. Without thinking she scooped up the pistol. It felt odd. Not what she expected a pistol to feel like but she didn't care at that very moment.

The man took a step toward Paul, knife held out, ready to do damage.

Lydia pointed the pistol at the man. "Who's stupid?" she asked, and fired.

The man had started to turn his head toward Lydia when a dart pierced his throat. His eyes widened. Then they went cross eyed and he dropped the knife.

He fell to his knees, clutching the dart in his neck. He made a strange gurgling noise, then pitched forward onto his face. Then he was still.

Paul looked from the man to Lydia, then to the man again.

"Wow," he said. "Thanks for that."

Lydia was staring at the man in shock. "I... I shot him. I shot someone." Her hands were shaking, and she dropped the pistol to the ground. What had she done?

Paul leaned over the man, cautiously. He scooped up the knife.

"Did I kill him?" Lydia heard herself ask. She never in her life thought she would have to ask that question. She stared down at the inert form of the man with growing apprehension.

Paul put his finger the man's neck. After a few moments he shook his head. "No. He's not dead at all. Just out cold."

Relief flooded through Lydia. Thank God. She wasn't a murderer. Still, the panic coursed through her veins and she found she could not stop shaking.

Paul was examining the dart that stuck out of the man's neck. "It some sort of knock out toxin. Not meant to kill. Just render you unconscious. Looks like it works really fast, too."

He picked up the pistol Lydia had dropped. "Just a dart gun. Can't fire bullets." He opened the pistol exposing an empty chamber. "Just a one shot affair. Not much use to us." He tossed it to the ground.

It was then he noticed Lydia shaking. He looked at her in concern. "Hey, easy there." He put his hands on her shoulders, like he had when they were in the closet. "He's not dead. Just asleep. You did the right thing. Trust me."

"Yeah," Lydia managed to say. His closeness was reassuring. She felt herself calm down. Her shaking subsided.

Paul pocketed the knife, and looked around. "Well, we can't stay around here. Best we stick to the plan."

"Plan?" Lydia asked dumbly. Was she still in a state of shock?

"Yeah," he said taking her hand again. "Running away."
Then they ran into the jungle.

Chapter 11

Oswald

This was not good.

Oswald stood at the bottom of the west wing fire escape, glaring up at the second floor's open door. They had been here. Morgan and the woman. He cast his gaze about the dense jungle that crowded around him. They could be anywhere by now.

Things were not going according to plan.

After landing, and an initial search of the buildings immediate to the docks, his men then moved to scour the main complex. It was huge with hundreds of rooms. But neither he, or his men would be deterred. Their prey was here. They just had to find him.

But once it was clear that the Billionaire had vanished his men started to get irritable. Hadn't he promised them an easy catch? Shouldn't they be at sea by now, heading to the next staging area, then off to the Philippines. At least there no one would find them amongst the thousand of islands in the chain.

It had not happened that way, but Oswald had remained firm. He had to remind himself these were paid mercenaries, not true loyal soldiers.

"Find him safely, and I will triple the bonus," he had announced. This had the desired effect, and the men were off again. And if Oswald was being honest with himself, he was relieved. If they did not find the Billionaire, and soon, he could be in trouble himself. Triple bonus or not.

Suddenly, Reeka appeared at the north corner of the building. "Sir!" he said, "You should see this."

"Did you find him?" Oswald asked, as he starting moving. That would be a relief.

"No," said Reeka. "But bad news."

Oswald fumed, but followed. They passed the huge resort balcony and then through a small maze of bungalows. There he found several of his men standing over another man, who was leaning against a wall.

"What is this?" Oswald demanded. "What happened to him?"

The man was groggy, almost drunk, and Oswald immediately suspected what had happened. When the man spoke, Reeka translated. "He saw Morgan with a woman leave out the fire escape. He gave chase, but when he came to this spot he was jumped. He said Morgan and him had a great fight, but Morgan managed to wrestle his dart gun away and shot him with it."

Oswald frowned down at the man. It sounded plausible. Then he had a realization. "Did you have a machine gun? Did he take it?"

The man shook his head. Reeka said, "Just a knife. He only had the dart gun."

"Here it is," said another mercenary, holding up the spent gun.

"Well at least he isn't armed with a machine gun," said Oswald. "That would make this far more difficult." He turned to look at the jungle canopy before them.

Thick, and choking. If Morgan wanted to hide he could do it in there. Oswald cursed himself inwardly for not bringing any heat vision equipment. There hadn't been any time.

If Morgan took to hiding then his men still had a chance of finding him. And if night fell, so be it. His men would wait until dawn and try again, but not for much longer. By then, someone would come looking for the Billionaire.

There was another potential wrinkle. One they did not really consider because the mission had appeared to be so easy at first.

"Are there any other docks on the island?" he asked Reeka.

The head mercenary considered. "Not on the last set of maps we have. But that doesn't mean there could be a simple boat left behind by a fishermen, or tourists."

This was a potential hazard. There was no way to secure the entire shoreline of the island from other people coming ashore. Instead, they had pinned their hopes on scooping up Morgan at the resort. Now, if there was a boat somewhere on a beach, he could get away, or at least get far enough out to sea to not be detected.

Oswald noticed the other men watching him think. He needed to stay the man of action. "Okay," he said, "we need to ensure he can't get off the island. We need to find any other boats and take care of them. Then, we flush him out."

He turned to Reeka. "Take some men and head up the east side of the island, and check the beaches. I'll take our boat and head around the west. We'll leave a guard behind here in case they double back. The rest of the men should search inland."

Reeka didn't react at first, but then turned and barked orders to the other men. They ran off into the jungle.

As Oswald turned to head back to the ship Reeka said, "We better find him soon. Boss."

Was that a scowl on his face? Oswald thought. Instead of getting angry, he said, "We will."

Reeka took some men and then headed into the jungle, going east.

Oswald walked back toward the dock. Reeka's disposition wasn't helping. Even dangerous, to a degree. But they would find that Billionaire soon.

Allowing himself to smile again Oswald just kept telling himself the same thought over and over in his mind.

There was no where Morgan could hide.

Chapter 12

Paul

The jungle was difficult, but they pushed through.

At the point they had entered there were no paths, so they had to scamper and climb around the thick foliage. The topography of the island was hilly, and the trees were very tall which kept them from seeing exactly where they were going.

But it also meant it was far more difficult for them to be followed.

As Paul pushed aside a thick set of branches for them to move past, Lydia sighed.

"I have to rest," she said, looking as tired as she sounded. "Can we risk a small break?" She then went over to a nearby fallen log and sat down.

Well, that settles it, Paul thought with a slight grin. He was tired, too. Dog tired. And we felt they could stop for a little while. They had been running for well over an hour non-stop. Their pursuers would probably be as lost as they were right now.

Paul sat beside her.

Lydia seemed to remember she was still carrying her day bag, and pulled out a half full bottle of water. She guzzled at it with relish.

Paul watched her. This was one impressive woman. She had kept her wits about her despite all that was happening. He worried she might have a break down, or worse, become totally paralysed with fear. Yet, she was keeping up with him with little complaint.

Lydia noticed him looking at her and offered the bottle. He took it and sipped.

"We should check our phones again. Just in case."

Still no signal for either of them.

"How long can they keep this up? Blocking the phones like this?" she said. Her face was sheened with sweat. Paul found himself thinking it made her look even more attractive.

"I really don't know," he answered. "Not really my area of expertise. But I do know they are working against the clock."

"Our people," Lydia said nodding.

"Yeah. Soon someone is going to start to wonder about us. And our would-be-kidnappers want to have use whisked away long before that."

"At least they don't want to kill you. They're use of the darts proves that," Lydia said.

But that doesn't rule out harm to you, Paul thought. He did not say it aloud. "Yeah, how kind of them."

Lydia eyes perked up. "Do you hear that?"

"What?"

They listened. Sure enough, there was a low rumbling noise coming from a short distance way.

"What is that?" Lydia said, perplexed.

"Sounds like water."

"We could use some," Lydia said, taking the empty bottle from him and putting it in her bag again.

"Let's take a look," he said and stood. He offered his hand to her, and she took it with a smile and stood.

"Such a gentleman," she said. "Even in all this."

"Gentleman to the end," he said and lead them further through the jungle.

They almost immediately came upon a break in the jungle. They stood on the edge of a wide river that snaked off into the jungle to their right. To their left was a large waterfall splashing loudly which fed into a pool, the source of the river.

For a moment they both were stunned by how beautiful the sight was. Such an unexpected thing to come across.

"This looks so inviting," said Lydia. "Do you think we have time for a bath?" She grinned.

It took a moment for Paul to realize that she was joking. "Maybe some other time. For now lets refill the water - ".

There was a distinct noise from behind them. They crouched and turned to look. Somewhere in the jungle something was moving toward them. Paul suspected it was more than one individual.

There was no time to head back into in the jungle and try to lose them. The only way to go was the water in front of them.

"Quick, hide your bag," he said, pointing to some thick bushes.

"Why?" she asked, but did as he said. She shoved her bag out of sight.

He took a few steps into the water. "Because were going to hide in that." He nodded toward the waterfall.

Lydia's eyes widened, but didn't protest. It wasn't like they had many options at this point. She stepped into the water, too.

"Stay under and swim behind the falls if you can," he said. He submerged himself up to his shoulders, the bottom of the river too deep to touch with his feet anymore.

"Okay," Lydia said. She took a few quick deep breaths then dove out of view.

Suddenly, at the jungle tree line, Paul saw several men push their way through.

With a quick breath, he dropped down fully into the water.

It was dark and murky. The water rushing into his ears and muffling his hearing. He looked about and saw Lydia swimming under water, frog style. She was a natural.

Paul followed suit, and soon was up next to her.

There were no gunshots or sounds of pursuit, not that they would really notice under here.

But the sound of the waterfall was all encompassing. As they approached the point of the water curtain hitting the river, white bubbles frothed their view.

They pushed under. He felt pressure against his head and body, then nothing. They had made it to the other side.

Paul raised his head up first and looked about. He was in a narrow gap between the falling curtain of water, and the rock wall behind it. Satisfied everything was okay, he used his hand to guide Lydia up.

She sputtered as she surfaced. They were both gasping for air. He wasn't sure how long they were under water, but it was obvious they had both reached their limit.

Then, through the sheet of water, Paul saw movement. It was hard to see through the falling water, but he could tell it was a person moving along the shore line.

Instinct took over and he pressed himself up to the corner of the little alcove, pulling Lydia along with him. When he could go no further he sunk down so just his head was above the water. Lydia did the same.

From here, he was certain they would not be spotted through the water, or in the little corner with just a small part of themselves exposed. But he couldn't count on miracles with so much at stake.

He pulled Lydia closer to him, and she hugged him almost eagerly. One arm around his shoulders, the other around his waist. He was tall enough to stand here, but she couldn't reach the bottom.

It was logical for her to cling to him like that. Yeah, that made sense, he thought to himself.

With apprehension they watched the figure move along the water's edge. It stopped, and whomever it was seemed to be looking around. Had he discovered the bag and put two and two together?

They waited with bated breath, unsure of what was going to happen. Would they be spotted? Would the person think of the waterfall as a hiding place?

After a few moments, the man started moving again. He was joined with another who seemed to materialize out of the jungle. They conferred briefly.

Then, to Lydia and his great relief, the two figures wondered further down the river and out of sight.

The two water born fugitives breathed a sigh. Lydia was still pressed against his body. She looked up to him and smiled.

He was again struck with how stunning she was. How beautiful.

He wasn't sure why, maybe it was the tenseness of the situation, or the danger which heightened his emotions but he felt a sudden and irresistible urge.

He pulled her closer, leaned down a little and kissed her.

Chapter 13

Lydia

To say that Lydia was surprised was an understatement.

When Paul had pulled her close while they were hiding, she did not offer a hint of complaint. In fact, she greatly enjoyed his closeness, despite the circumstance. She felt safe, hidden away behind the waterfall but she felt even more so when she clung to Paul.

Then he had to go and kiss her.

At first, her eyes widened in shock, but she did not resist. Then, when her brain was processing what was happening, she reacted. She kissed him back.

For several long, water drenched moments they did not part, lips locked together. The only thing that registered of the outside world was the splashing of the waterfall.

She wasn't sure how long they remained like that, but eventually they stopped. They both grinned at each other like high school sweethearts.

I did not want him to stop, she thought. But maybe later. If there was one.

Paul started to say something. His lips moved but she couldn't hear anything over the rumbling of the water.

He laughed, and so did she. Both sounds drowned out in the splashing around them.

Paul grabbed her hand, and nodded in the direction of the water fall. He wanted them to leave.

Lydia was genuinely afraid. Armed men were out there. And they didn't want to do nice things to them. Yet, they couldn't stay here. It was quite possible this spot would eventually be checked. Or they would go deaf waiting here for rescue.

Paul took a deep breath then eased under the water, not letting go of her hand. Lydia followed suit. Beneath the surface they swam, hand in hand. It was a little awkward but it gave Lydia a little comfort.

They passed under the water fall, but instead of swimming on, Paul pointed up. She understood.

Inch by inch they surfaced until up past their noses. The water churned around them, so close to the falls. If she reached out she could touch it.

Paul and Lydia scanned the river's edge. Jungle, jungle and more jungle. They looked over it all, slowly tracking across their field of vision. No one was around.

Carefully, they swam back to the spot they first submerged, ready to plunge under the surface at the first sign of trouble. They slunk out of the water, dripping wet. As Paul kept watch, Lydia fetched her bag from the bushes. She was relieved to find it still there. It hadn't been discovered, thankfully.

"Which way?" she asked. She found she was standing close to him. Closer than she normally would have.

Paul looked about. "Best we head in the opposite direction those two did. That would still put us in the same direction we were walking in. But I really think we need to avoid the river."

"To easy to spot us walking along it."

"Yeah, or even swimming in it. Not worth the risk. No, we should continue on, but head back into the jungle. Maybe find a place hide and wait this out."

"I liked our hiding spot," Lydia said and smiled.

Paul focused on her, and smiled back. "I liked it, too. But if they come back this way, it would be the most obvious place to check."

As he spoke, his eyes roamed over her face; her eyes, her lips, her nose. Lydia was starting to get a little flustered. But in a good way.

Then, again by complete surprise, Paul leaned forward and kissed her on the lips.

Lydia kissed back, then laughed. "What was that for?"

Taking her hand, he said, "For luck. Now let's go."

Together they reentered the jungle. But Lydia felt distinctly different than before.

Chapter 14

Paul

They pushed on through the jungle, the terrain doing everything in its power to slow them down. But they couldn't stop. It wasn't safe, and they hadn't come across anything that would be considered a good hiding spot.

"Do you think we lost them completely?" Lydia asked.

Paul shook his head. "Hard to know, for sure. They certainly aren't going to stop looking for us. Probably will do so right up until the last second."

"Until rescue comes," Lydia said pushing branches out of her way. It was getting more difficult to move.

"Yes, whoever that would be."

"Who do you think? The coast guard?"

Paul paused for a second, considering. "I want the United States Navy to show up. That would be cool."

Lydia laughed. "Yeah, we can only wish. With our luck it will be a local police patrol boat. They also double as fishing trawlers around these parts."

They both laughed. Paul found himself enjoying her presence more and more. There was certainly a connection between them. He hoped that after all this nonsense was over, he would be given a chance to see if something more would become of it.

Even if it didn't, there was no denying the fact he was fast developing feelings for this beautiful woman. Perhaps it was the dire situation they had been thrown in together, or the dang heat playing with his head. Either way, it felt good. She could very well be a potential keeper.

He found he was smiling at her, not saying anything.

Lydia arched a quizzical brow and smiled back. "Something the matter?"

"If your not counting being chased by a gang of pirates something the matter, then no. Nothing is the matter."

They laughed again.

Suddenly, someone shouted at them.

Paul and Lydia turned to look.

Two men stood on the other side of a rocky outcropping, looking directly at them from a short distance away. Both were carrying machine guns.

"Oh, God," Lydia said.

Paul noticed both men had their machine guns pointed directly at him. Then, one man spoke to the other. The men changed their target from Paul to Lydia.

"Get down!" Paul shouted and jumped.

He pulled Lydia down to the ground at the very instant the tree she was standing in front of exploded. Bullets riddled the trunk, bark flying everywhere.

Lydia was shouting, but Paul was already moving. He dragged her further down the slight incline they were following. Getting her out of the way.

The firing stopped. The men were shouting again. Coming for them, trying to scramble over the rocky outcropping.

Paul pulled Lydia up, her eyes were wide with fear. "Run!" he said.

They ran. Tearing through the jungle, branches whipped at their faces and arms. Paul was keeping Lydia directly in front of her. He didn't want her to be an easy target.

They tried to kill her, he thought. Because of me, they tried to kill her.

Behind them were more shouts, but he couldn't tell how close they were. Yet there was no denying it. They had been good as spotted. Soon the men would find them.

And they would kill Lydia.

As if a curtain was ripped aside, they broke through the jungle. Lydia gasped and stumbled. Paul grabbed her at the last moment.

They were on the edge of a ravine. It was just a little to wide for them to try jumping across. It was maybe thirty feet deep, with sheer walls at its sides.

"Well this isn't good," Lydia said.

Paul glanced in both directions. With the jungle pressed in so close to them it was impossible to see how long it was. Which direction should they go now?

Then Lydia's face brightened. "I know this from my research. There's a rope bridge, somewhere here."

"Where?" Paul asked, looking behind them. He could hear their pursuers crashing through the brush.

Lydia pointed to their left. "This way. Come on!"

Scrambling along the ravine's edge was difficult, plus navigating the trees and bushes that insisted on leaning over, blocking their way.

Within moments he saw something ahead of them, spanning the ravine.

"There it is!" Lydia said, elated.

But as they got closer Paul felt whatever relief he thought he should have at that moment evaporate. It wasn't a normal bridge. It was a rope bridge. One thick rope to walk on, with two others on either side to hold onto. Not ideal. And it looked old and neglected.

"Doesn't look really safe," Paul said as they hurried up to it.

"Well, it's not like we have many options at the moment," Lydia said. She grabbed one of the hand ropes and shook it. The entire sagging bridge wiggled, but appeared to be secure.

Somewhere behind them were voices, men calling to one another.

"We gotta go," Lydia said.

"Ladies first," Paul said, with a tight smile.

"Such a gentleman," she said, grinning. She looked almost giddy. All this running and adrenaline was making them act a little goofy.

"Always," he said, and meant it. Right to the end, he thought.

Lydia stepped out onto the rope. If wiggled about under her weight but after a few steps, seemed to settle a bit.

Paul watched Lydia navigate her way across, his mind already made up what he had to do. This couldn't go on any longer. If it was just him running around the jungle, he would be fine with trying to evade these men. But not with Lydia. She would always be in terrible danger right up until rescue arrived. If it did arrive.

When Lydia was almost across Paul withdrew the knife from his pocket. It was the one he took from the man he had tackled.

He heard the men in the jungle getting closer. They would arrive in moments. Even if he started to cross the rope bridge now he wouldn't make it.

Placing the knife against one of the hand ropes, he tightened his grip. Cutting both hand ropes would effectively keep anyone else from crossing. He hoped that would be enough of a deterrent to their pursuers that they would not go after Lydia.

Lydia had said that crossing this bridge was their only option, but she was not correct. There was one more option, and only Paul could do it.

The very moment Lydia stepped onto the solid ground on the other side, Paul started cutting.

Lydia turned, to look at him. Immediately her expression changed from one of hope to horror.

Just at that moment, the two men burst out of the jungle directly behind him.

"What are you doing?" Lydia called out. She looked shocked.

The rope cut. Paul quickly turned his attention to the other hand rope and started cutting. Out of the corner of his eye he could see the men running up to him, shouting something angrily in their language.

Just as he cut the second rope, he sensed the men were upon him.

The butt of a gun caught him in the side of the head. The world exploded in color, and he tumbled to the ground.

Lydia was still shouting, but he couldn't tell what it was. It didn't matter. She had to go. Now!

"Run! Run and hide!" Paul shouted. He felt wetness stream down the side of his face.

One of the men was at the ravine's edge, next to the now solo rope that spanned it. He levelled his gun across, pointing it at Lydia.

"No!" Paul shouted. He found himself moving, crashing into the other other man.

The machine gun fired.

Chapter 15

Lydia

Lydia was screaming even as she dove for cover. Bullets passed by her like lethal angry insects intent on her death. She scrambled into the jungle, trying to get away from the shooting.

She hugged the ground, laying as flat as she could.

The shooting had stopped.

What had happened to Paul?

Slowly, unsure of what was happening, she crawled back toward the ravine. Once she was close, and sure she hadn't been observed, she parted some leaves.

There, across the ravine, were the two men. They had hoisted Paul up from the ground. Even from this distance she could tell he had been hurt. Shot?

No. There was blood along the right side of his face. Had he been hit?

Thankfully, the men no longer gave Lydia any regard. Instead, they turned their backs to the ravine, and with Paul wobbling between them, moved off into the jungle.

Oh, my God, she thought. They got him. No, that was entirely true. He had given himself up to them. To save her. That was the only explanation for his insane behaviour, cutting the ropes on the bridge.

It kept the men from crossing after her, but it prevented Paul from crossing, too. He had sacrificed himself for her safety.

The fool! She thought, tears welling in her eyes. The handsome, wonderful fool!

Get a hold of yourself, girl. You have to do something. You can't just let them take him away, whether that was Paul's intention or not. It wasn't going to happen. Not on her watch.

She wiped tears away from her eyes and face. She needed to follow them. Somehow. If they got away from her, she would never have an opportunity to help. Whatever that mysterious help may be.

Okay, that's what she would do. Follow them. But first, she had to get around this ravine. She turned toward the east, since she sensed it was the closest direction to the edge of the island and pushed through the jungle.

Soon, she passed the ravine entirely, and trudged on. It was only after a short while that she realized she no longer had her day bag. She must have dropped it when the man was shooting at her. She shrugged. Nothing she could do about it now. She kept going.

She must of been marching through the jungle for a good twenty minutes when she noticed a change in her surroundings. Through the trees, in the distance she could now see the ocean. She had made it to the east side of the island. At least she had an idea where she was.

Turning north, she resumed her trek. She hoped that the men would not march Paul all the way back to the resort. Instead, there was a good chance they may pick him up at a nearby beach. If she got there in time maybe she could do something.

But what?

As if on cue the trees ahead of her thinned out. She could see a long white beach extend out in front of her, which was nestled up against a little cove.

Not here, she thought glumly. But as she started to turn away, her eyes caught movement.

Peering through the trees she could see two men walk onto the beach, way down at the other end. They had Paul between them. She felt her heart leap in her chest. He was alive, and mostly unharmed.

The three men stopped, looking out to sea. Lydia turned to look. She saw a large ship pulling into the little cove a short distance away. At first she thought it might be a rescue ship of some sort, but that thought quickly vanished when she recognized it.

It was the same one that had arrived at the dock back at the resort. The pirate's ship.

Still, she had to do something. What it was she did not have the foggiest notion. She started walking toward the beach.

"Ah," someone said. "There you are."

Lydia stopped in her tracks, just as a man stepped out from behind a large tree right beside her.

They looked at each other.

"Who is stupid?" The man asked. "You are. And I'm going to teach you some manners. Yes?"

Lydia was shocked. It was the man Paul had tackled back at the resort. The man she had shot.

He didn't look much worse for wear for someone who had been rendered unconscious a few hours earlier. He did have a huge red welt on his neck from the dart. But he was up and about now.

And he was right here.

Lydia's eyes went to the submachine gun he held in both hands, pointed at her. She noticed he had another dart pistol holstered on his hip.

"You found me," Lydia said, trying to buy some time. She needed a plan. They were taking Paul away. She couldn't afford to waste time on this idiot.

The man took a few steps toward her. He leered at her with his half toothed smile. "I think for a stupid woman you are pretty. Pretty enough to make me happy, huh?"

Dread washed over Lydia. Ice shot up her spine. This was going to get ugly, and quick if she didn't do something. But what?

As entered her personal space, she cowered in fright. He had been shorter than Paul, but was still a couple of inches taller than her. He was very wiry, and he stunk to high heaven.

"You make me feel good, maybe I let you live, huh?" He licked his lips. His eyes raked over her body hungrily. Her legs, her breasts, her mouth. It made Lydia shudder in revulsion.

"I... I think I understand," Lydia said. She allowed her look of fright to slowly morph to one of appeasement. She tried to smile at him.

"That is a good girl. Stupid, yes. But maybe good for us both," he said. Now unable to contain himself he started to grab at her, pulling her up against him.

Lydia endured it. He kissed at her neck and groped at her body. She even embraced him, rubbing up against his wiry frame. He was excited to the point of bursting.

"That's a good girl," he said, breathing harsh smelly air into her ear.

After a moment, Lydia stood upright and looked directly into the man's face, bare inches away.

He was surprised, but scowled. "What is this? Stupid woman tricks?"

"I have a question for you, you handsome devil," she grinned at him.

Genuinely perplexed the man said, "What question?"

Lydia shot him in the groin.

The man gasped in pain and pulled back from her. He gaped down at the little dart that protruded from his crotch.

"Who is stupid?" Lydia asked.

The man then looked at her in complete surprise. Then he went cross-eyed, and fell to his knees. He made some sort of keening noise, then pitched forward into the dirt face first.

Lydia allowed herself a moment of satisfaction. Letting this cretin feel her up gave her the opportunity to take the pistol from him. So intent on drooling over her flesh, the idiot didn't even notice.

She cast the spent pistol aside, then quickly bent down over the man. Mr. Smelly was snoring loudly in the dirt. She managed to pull the submachine gun out from under his still form.

She stood, examining it. This was exactly what she needed.

"Thanks for this," she said to the unconscious man.

She looked back down the beach again. To her relief, Paul was still there with his captors. The ship had dropped anchor and a small motor boat was making its way across the cove towards Paul. There were a couple of men on it. They were coming to take Paul away.

Not going to happen, she thought.

She hefted the submachine gun in her grip, and started hurrying toward the beach. She was going to show these idiots what an angry, armed Realtor would do to protect a client.

She was going to rescue Paul.

Chapter 16

Paul

Lydia was safe, Paul thought. That was all that mattered now. They wouldn't pursue her anymore. They got what they wanted.

He tried to ease his worry with these thoughts as the two men half dragged him through the jungle. He had tackled the one that had been shooting and he stopped almost immediately. It was obvious they could not risk Paul getting seriously injured. They seemed to settle on just scowling at him, and cursing in their language.

At some point they paused. One of them was speaking into a handset of some sort. Something short range, modulated so as not to be effected by their jamming device.

Orders came over it, and they changed their course. Instead of heading north, back to the resort he assumed, they were heading east. Probably to the shore to be picked up.

And then what? Whisked away to some unknown island not much different than this one. Chained up and thrown in hole? They would demand money, that was for certain. He would play along with them. His security firm, once they realized he was kidnapped, would leap into action. And those guys were good. It could be that they could home in on his position and attempt a rescue.

If it was a success, he would give them all a bonus.

But then his attention would turn to the only thing on his mind: Lydia. He would follow up with her, sending his security team to the island to scour it for her.

He prayed she was safe, and unharmed. He also hoped she had enough sense to stay far enough away from him right now. No sense them both getting caught. Or worse.

He and his captors suddenly arrived at a beach. Pure white powdery sand stretched off down the shore almost out of sight.

But his eyes caught movement out at sea. It was a ship, the one the pirates were using. Great. This was it.

The two men pushed him to his knees in the sand. Paul sagged. They had long before tied his hands together with twine, which cut into his wrists. He did not even have the energy to try and break them. Best to save his energy for whatever the future presented to him.

A boat left the ship, and headed toward the beach. Paul could make out two men on board. One didn't look Filipino. Maybe a Westerner, or European.

Paul closed his eyes. He would know soon enough. Instead, he listened to the waves lapping at the beach, and thought of Lydia's face, smiling up at him from behind the waterfall.

The boat arrived, and the two men disembarked. The Westerner was tall, and commanding in presence. He grinned down at Paul, almost wild in his look.

"Mr. Morgan, I presume?" the new arrival said, and then laughed at his own joke.

Paul frowned at him. "I know you?"

"Not formally, no. My name is Oswald. And I am your captor of the day." The grin never left his face. There was a glint in his eye. It was the look of absolute greed. And he was looking down at Paul, his treasure.

"Looks like you got yourself a major payday in your future," Paul said. He found himself working at the twine around his wrists. Like it would do much good now.

The man called Oswald laughed. "I am hoping it would be a sizable one."

Paul looked up at him, sunlight causing him to squint. "Whatever it is, I could ensure it would be double that amount."

Oswald looked pleasantly shocked. "Why, isn't that kind of you. Whatever would you want in return for this generous offer?"

"Leave the woman alone," Paul said. "The one that was with me. If your men are still looking for her, tell them to stop now. And if they caught here, let her go. Do this one thing and I will promise that the ransom paid to you would exceed your wildest dreams."

Oswald laughed, more with delight than anything. "A woman? You would cough up untold hundreds of millions for a woman?"

Play to his greed, Paul thought. "That is the offer."

Oswald seemed to consider it. Then he turned and asked one of the men a question in what sounded to be very broken Tagalog. The man shook his head.

Oswald looked at Paul again. "It would appear that this woman of yours is evading my men. But, I accept your offer. We will cease searching for her immediately. Good enough?"

Paul nodded.

As if basking in his own glory, Oswald sniffed and grinned. "A woman. Ha! She had been nothing more than an annoyance. But I see now that she was useful to me after all. Her presence got me you."

Oswald laughed. The other henchman laughed along with him. What did they care? They were rich now. Richer than they could ever dream.

"Now you've really gone and ticked me off!" Someone shouted.

Everyone jumped in surprise and stopped laughing. They turned toward the voice.

Paul gasped in shock.

Lydia emerged slowly from the jungle directly behind them, only a few feet away. To Paul's amazement, she was armed with a submachine gun, which she had leveled at Oswald.

He also noticed something else about her. She was mad. Real mad.

Everyone tensed. When she emerged, all the men either had their weapons holstered, or slung over their shoulders. They hadn't expected any armed conflict standing here.

Lydia had caught them all completely by surprise.

Paul beamed at her.

"What? What is this?" Oswald said, stunned.

Lydia stopped moving, standing with her legs slightly apart, the submachine gun firmly levelled, finger on the trigger. "What is this? The end of the line for you idiots. Now, drop your weapons."

Paul could feel the tension rising amongst the group. Did they think the could get the drop on her? Would she even fire at them? He could sense these thoughts racing through their minds.

They were killers, mostly all. But not Lydia. Did she have what it took to kill someone here and now?

Oswald seemed to regain some of his composure. "Now, look miss, I don't know what you were thinking coming here, but this game is over. Drop the weapon and I swear you won't be hurt."

"Yeah, I believe you," she said. She hoisted the gun up a little higher. "I said drop your weapons. All of you."

Now Oswald had worked up enough bravado that he obviously felt he could call her bluff. "You aren't going to shoot anyone. You don't have it in you, do you now? Now, put down that gun and we'll - ."

Lydia shot at Oswald.

The noise was deafening as it was sudden. Paul blinked as sand shot up from the beach.

No, she didn't shoot Oswald, but she had shot a line through the sand between him and one of the other men.

A feeling of unease grew amongst the men.

"Drop them. I will not repeat myself," she said.

She had said it so angrily, that if Paul were carrying a gun at that moment, he would have dropped it, too.

Oswald scowled. "Drop them. Everyone."

Slowly, and under her very watchful gaze, the men dropped their weapons in the sand.

"Now untie him," she said.

Oswald nodded to one of the men, who bent down and quickly undid his bindings. Once free, Paul stood, rubbing at his wrists.

"Well this is a pleasant surprise," Paul said, grinning wildly.

Lydia's features softened a little as she glanced at him. "Well, we can talk about that later. Grab a gun now, honey."

"Oh," Paul said. "Right." He selected a machine gun from the ample pile then walked over to stand by Lydia.

They both looked at their new prisoners, who stood with shoulders slumped in defeat.

"Now what should we do with them?" Paul asked.

"I dunno," Lydia said with a slight shrug. "I was hoping at some point now the cavalry would arrive."

"Cavalry?" Paul said.

There was a distant rumbling. Everyone looked about, blinking in confusion.

"What the hell?" Paul said.

Just then a helicopter shot over the jungle canopy and passed above them.

Stunned, the only thing everyone on the beach could do was stare in surprise.

The huge machine banked hard, and lowered a bit over the water right next to the beach. The water sprayed outwards, and kicked up sand.

A uniformed soldier hung out an open side hatch, a massive mounted gun pointed down at them.

Paul blinked at the lettering along the side of the helicopter. United States Navy.

Paul blinked in amazement. "Well, I'll be damned!" he said.

Lydia and Paul laughed.

Chapter 17

Lydia

"You knew my paranoia would pay off in spades, one day, didn't you, sister mine?" Mary said, her image crisp and clear on Paul's phone. Now that the jammer was off, Lydia was able to call Mary.

And Lydia was very happy to see her.

"How did you know we were in trouble?" Lydia asked. She glanced up at the beach.

The chopper had landed on the beach, and marines had secured the prisoners. In the distance, a United States Navy frigate had just made anchor not far from Oswald's own boat.

Mary laughed. "My dear, when you said you had something very, very important to tell me, and that I had to listen, only then to have the connection cut off, I suspected something was amiss. I tried your number many times. And when that didn't work, I tried Paul's phone. And when that didn't work I went into full panic mode. I called his assistant, who called someone in the government, who contacted the navy, and, well, there you are."

Lydia grinned at her sister. "Sister, mine. You can be as paranoid as you want. Don't ever stop." Lydia glanced up to see Paul talking to one of the marines. He then started to walk over to her.

"So tell me," Mary said, her voice all conspiratorial. "Is he handsome or what?"

"Who's that?" Paul said, walking over to stand next to Lydia.

"Oh!" Mary cried in surprise.

Lydia laughed and pointed the phone at Paul. "Paul, this is my sister Mary. Mary this is Paul Morgan. He's very talented at cutting ropes."

"Nice to meet you Mary. And thanks for bringing us the cavalry," Paul said, smiling into the phone. Lydia knew the effect this would have on her sister.

"Oh, my!" Mary said. "Such a pleasure to meet you... Oh, ropes? Cutting? What are you not telling me, Lydia!"

Lydia and Paul both laughed.

"I'll call you once we make it back to the main island. I promise."

"Of, course. Take your time, I understand. But, you must know, I am absolutely starving for details!" Mary said.

"And you will get them," Lydia said. "Bye for now." She signed off and looked to Paul. He looked a lot more relaxed than he had a short while ago, tied up on the beach.

Paul smiled at her. "They're searching the island for Oswald's other men. I don't think it will be much of a problem for these guys." He looked over at the marines who were now loading the prisoners onto the chopper.

Oswald was about to step on board when he looked in Lydia and Paul's direction. He grimaced.

Lydia waved, and Oswald vanished into the helicopter.

"Now what?" she asked Paul.

He stepped closer to her, and eased his arms around her. She liked it. She really liked it. He beamed down at her.

"Well, I think we have some unfinished business to attend to."

Lydia's eyes widened in surprise. "Really? After all of this, you still want this island?"

Paul blinked, then looked around at the jungle as if seeing this place for the first time. "Oh, yeah. Right." He looked back down at her. "I just consider the island a bonus. I already found what I really wanted."

Lydia smiled at him.

Then he leaned forward and they kissed.

END

Also by Winter Hayles

Tropical Trouble
Caine: Redux Edition: Bad Boy MC Romance

www.ingramcontent.com/pod-product-compliance
Ingram Content Group UK Ltd.
Pitfield, Milton Keynes, MK11 3LW, UK
UKHW021935190726
13853UKWH00004B/1458

9 798201 114701